ARCTIC THUNDER

ARCTIC
THUNDER

a novel

ROBERT FEAGAN

DUNDURN PRESS
TORONTO

Editor: Michael Carroll
Design: Jennifer Scott
Printer: Webcom

Library and Archives Canada Cataloguing in Publication

Feagan, Robert, 1959-
          Arctic thunder / by Robert Feagan.

ISBN 978-1-55488-700-2

I. Title.

PS8561.E18A73 2010   jC813'.54   C2009-907537-7

1   2   3   4   5   14   13   12   11   10

 Conseil des Arts du Canada   Canada Council for the Arts Canadä ONTARIO ARTS COUNCIL
CONSEIL DES ARTS DE L'ONTARIO

We acknowledge the support of the **Canada Council for the Arts** and the **Ontario Arts Council** for our publishing program. We also acknowledge the financial support of the **Government of Canada** through the **Canada Book Fund** and **The Association for the Export of Canadian Books**, and the **Government of Ontario** through the **Ontario Book Publishers Tax Credit** program, and the **Ontario Media Development Corporation**.

Care has been taken to trace the ownership of copyright material used in this book. The author and the publisher welcome any information enabling them to rectify any references or credits in subsequent editions.

J. Kirk Howard, President

Printed and bound in Canada.
www.dundurn.com

Dundurn Press	Gazelle Book Services Limited	Dundurn Press
3 Church Street, Suite 500	White Cross Mills	2250 Military Road
Toronto, Ontario, Canada	High Town, Lancaster, England	Tonawanda, NY
M5E 1M2	LA1 4XS	U.S.A. 14150

99%   **ANCIENT FOREST** ™
FRIENDLY

*To Mike and all of the incredible athletes
who have played our first national sport in
the shadow of that other Canadian pastime.
And to the memory of Victor Allen.*

ACKNOWLEDGEMENTS

I would like to thank Loretta Trimble Hopkins and Gerry Kisoun for their contributions to the background information in *Arctic Thunder*. I would also like to thank the Kisoun and Allen families for providing information on Victor Allen and allowing me to pay tribute to his memory through his character in the novel.

CHAPTER 1

Mike stood at centre floor and bent forward at the waist, resting his stick across his thighs. Staring down, he watched as a bead of sweat slowly rolled the length of his nose and dropped through the cage of his helmet, plopping onto the smooth concrete floor. He took a deep breath, then exhaled with force as he straightened and glanced at the clock.

Forty seconds left in the third and final period. Red Deer Chiefs 7, St. Albert Rams 7. Mike shook his head in frustration and disbelief. It should never have come to this. They had been leading Red Deer 7–3 with four minutes left. That was before the roof caved in and the Chiefs roared back. Sure, it was box lacrosse and the tempo could swing in either direction in a finger snap, but this was the provincial final and St. Albert was a better team than this.

"Ref! Time out!" Mike's father, Ben Watson, who coached the team, was standing on the bench, wildly motioning to the referee with the palm of his left hand across the fingertips of his right hand in the shape of a T. The official blew his whistle and motioned to the timekeeper that the Rams had a twenty-second time-out. Mike shuffled toward the bench.

"Hustle up, hustle up!" Ben shouted to his team as they moved in close to their coach. "This is it, guys. This is our whole season, right here and now. Ryan, Cayln, Mike, Spencer, Scott, you're on the floor. Ryan, you have to win this one. Go for a drawback between your legs. Mike and Cayln, you know where the ball's going. Be there. Once we get possession, don't panic. Set up in their end and use the full thirty-second clock. If we can use the full clock, or get a shot and a reset before we score, then they won't have anything to work with. And, guys, believe me —" he paused and looked right at Mike "— we *are* going to score. Run play number three. Spencer, that means you move in for that pick. Have you got it?" The boys all nodded. The referee whistled behind them, signalling the timeout was over. "All right, guys, put it in and, Rams, let's win!"

The boys stuck out an arm with their gloves pressed together. "One, two, three, *Rams*!" they shouted.

Mike walked to his position just outside the centre faceoff circle, his frustration replaced by a sense of anger and purpose. He was competitive by nature and burned inside when he thought how they had squandered their lead. His dad was right. They were going to win this.

Ryan Domino was one of the best point men Mike had ever seen. Nine times out of ten he won the faceoff and sent the ball in the direction they planned. Scott Sutherland and Spencer Lorenz were both big and strong but more offensive than average shooters. Scott had taken up lacrosse later than most of the boys, but his mature build and strength made him a dominant force on the defensive side of the ball. Spencer's father, Todd, had played for the New Westminster Salmonbellies, had nine national championships, and had been inducted into the Canadian Lacrosse Hall of Fame. Spencer was the most naturally talented player Mike had ever seen.

Cayln Butz was fast and had a knack for getting open no matter what. With him on the opposite crease position, it had proven to be a great combination for scoring plenty of goals this season. Even though the majority of their players were only thirteen and first-year bantams like Mike, they had been one of the best teams in Alberta. This was the time to prove it.

A Chiefs player pushed himself in front of Mike, who shoved him back. They briefly jostled for position, but it didn't matter. Mike knew the ball would go to his right and that he would spin away at the whistle and run in that direction. Cayln would come from the other side of the ball.

Ryan and the opposing point man from the Chiefs knelt in the faceoff circle and put the baskets of their sticks back to back. The referee carefully placed the ball between the mesh of their sticks and slowly backed away, hand raised, whistle poised in his lips. The crowd yelled and clapped. Then the whistle blew, and the outside world vanished as Ryan pushed down hard on his stick and drew the ball between his feet.

At the whistle Mike used the Chiefs player as leverage and raced past him, heading to the right of the faceoff circle. He saw the ball spin out behind Ryan between his legs and bounce toward the boards on that side. Cayln, Mike, and two Chiefs players arrived together in a flurry of sticks, bodies, pushing, and shoving. Mike fell hard but spied Cayln emerging from the cluster as he scooped up the ball. Twisting from the pack with the ball, Cayln ran toward his own end, passed the ball to Spencer, then turned and loped quickly into the Red Deer zone.

"Set it up, set it up!" Spencer shouted behind Mike as he travelled into the Red Deer zone. Cayln shifted to the corner just left of the Chiefs' net, and Mike veered to the opposite side. Spencer and Scott set up high as Ryan moved just outside the goalie's crease. The Red Deer players set up in a defensive box, sticks held high, keeping the Rams to the outside and away from the net.

Spencer pretended to pass to Cayln, then got the ball over to Scott, who took a few steps in. After faking a shot, Scott passed the ball back to Spencer. Twenty seconds left on the shot clock. Ryan went down in front of the net as a Chiefs player checked him hard with a stick across the left arm. Spencer feigned a pass back to Scott but instead bounced the ball in to Cayln in the corner. Fifteen seconds left on the shot clock.

Ryan scrambled to his feet and moved to the left side of the net toward Cayln. "Three, three!" Ben cried frantically from the bench. Spencer ran in and planted himself beside the defender covering Cayln, who tried to dodge past but was blocked by another Chief. Cayln shifted back to the corner. Trapped! The play wasn't going to work. Eight seconds left on the shot clock.

With Cayln stuck in the corner, Mike lunged as if he were going to deke in front of the net. Instead he spun and raced behind the net from the right side. Five seconds on the shot clock.

"Now, now!" Mike shouted as he came around the left side of the net. With two Chiefs sticks held high in front of him, Cayln threw the ball between them in desperation. The ball came out too far ahead of Mike. Never taking his eyes off the ball, Mike stretched out, and as the ball hit the top of the pocket of his stick, he turned it and fired at the net in one quick-stick motion. A Chiefs player hit him from behind as the ball left his stick, sending him sprawling across the floor.

Landing face down, Mike heard the crowd roar. Before he could even think about looking at the net, hands grabbed him from all directions. Cayln and Spencer pulled him to his feet as Scott and Ryan threw their arms around his neck.

"Yaa!" Spencer yelled in his face.

"What a goal!" Ryan shouted.

Realizing he had scored, Mike pumped both his arms in the air, the adrenaline rush washing over him as he yelled at the rafters. *"Yaaaaaaaa!"*

The boys ran in a group toward the bench where they were mobbed by their teammates. Smiling, Ben caught Mike's attention and nodded in approval.

Once more the referee blew his whistle and pointed at the Red Deer bench. "Timeout, Chiefs!" Eleven seconds left in the game.

"In, in, in!" Ben ordered his players, motioning

ARCTIC THUNDER

once more for them to gather around. "Okay, here we
go. There's eleven seconds left. This is where we shut
them down. Ryan, I want you to stay on and win this
one. Spencer, you stay out. Taylor with Spence. Brady
and Cayln. If we win the draw, be sure to get over half
and rag that ball. If they get the ball, man on man. Stick
close and keep them out of our house. Are we ready?"

"You bet!" the boys shouted.

"Again, guys, put it in and do it," Ben told them.
"Rams!"

The boys put their gloves together. "One, two,
three, *Rams!*"

Mike moved to the end of the bench. He was
still pumped from his goal but ready to burst inside,
wanting the next eleven seconds to be done. Brady
Reid was a small player but incredibly fast and a tena-
cious checker. Taylor Fraser was a big boy and an
incredible all-round player. With his size and ability to check, it made sense to have him on the floor.
They had to win this.

Spencer, Cayln, Brady, Taylor, and Ryan walked
to their positions on the floor, determination in their
faces.

"Kirk!" Ben shouted at Kirk Miles, the Rams'
goalie. "Keep your head in the game. Only eleven seconds left." He pointed at the clock.

Tall and big for his age, Kirk looked like a real-life version of the Michelin Man in his goalie equipment. He nodded at Ben and whacked his stick against his goalie pads as he backed into the net. Nervously, he shifted from side to side, rapidly hitting each post with his stick.

The Chiefs' net was empty. Six attackers on the floor. They lined up with four players in the St. Albert end, one man in the faceoff circle, and only one man halfway back toward their own goal. With eleven seconds remaining, they had nothing to lose and had to pull out all the stops.

Spencer, Taylor, and Brady spaced themselves out in the St. Albert zone. Ryan lined up in the faceoff circle, with Cayln poised on the Chiefs' side of the ball. Once again Ryan knelt with the Chiefs' point man as the referee placed the ball between the heads of their sticks. Slowly backing away, the referee held his hand high as he checked both ends to make sure the teams were ready.

The noise was unbelievable. The game was at the Bill Hunter Arena in Edmonton, but both teams had huge followings in the stands. The building was filled to capacity, and each and every fan was standing, clapping and stomping as they shouted with all their might.

The players on each bench held their sticks over the boards and banged the aluminum shafts against the painted wood. Mike's heart was in his mouth as he joined his teammates, smacking his stick and shouting until all he could do was croak. He felt two hands tightly grip his shoulders from behind near his neck until it almost hurt. Glancing back, he found his father lost in the moment, staring out at the floor, oblivious to the fact he was about to strangle his son. Barely audible above the noise, the referee blew his whistle as he dropped his arm.

Ryan and the Chiefs' point man leaned on their sticks hard, struggling to draw the ball from the circle to direct it to their waiting teammates. With one last push, Ryan pulled the ball under the head of his stick and whipped it once again back and between his feet. This time, however, a Chiefs player was waiting. Eight seconds left.

Scooping the ball quickly off the floor, the Chiefs player immediately threw a long pass directly to his teammate in the corner of the Rams' zone. Six seconds left. Cayln and Ryan were racing to the Rams' zone to join their teammates as the Chief in the corner passed the ball out to a shooter waiting high in the zone. Four seconds. The shooter passed the ball deep to the opposite corner of the Rams' zone where once more a Chiefs player deftly caught the ball. Briefly hesitating, he spotted the shooter who had just passed the ball racing to the front of the net. With one step, he threw the ball — a perfect pass! As the ball sank into the webbing of the shooter's stick, he released the shot in an effortless motion. The ball zipped toward the top corner of the Rams' net. Caught off guard at the other side of the net, Kirk threw himself across but only caught part of the ball with his shoulder. It skipped off, popped into the crossbar, and with a thud hit the Plexiglas behind the net as the buzzer sounded to end the game.

The Rams' bench exploded. Sticks, gloves, and helmets flew in all directions as the players charged from the bench. With a whoop, Kirk threw off his gloves and mask and braced himself for the mob bearing down on him. In one crazy cluster, the team launched themselves onto their goalie until they fell in a giddy heap in front of the net. Slightly behind the other players, with a scream, Mike threw himself on top of the pile. The St. Albert fans clapped and yelled loudly from the stands as the Red Deer faithful politely applauded, heartbroken but proud of their players at the same time.

In a happy daze, Ben shook the hand of Barry Butz, the team's other coach and Cayln's father. Then they walked toward the delirious gang of players celebrating in front of their net. Spencer emerged from the mob and charged the coaches, spraying them with a water bottle as they put their hands up to protect themselves. Barry lunged and grabbed Spencer, while Ben tore the water bottle out of the boy's hands and spurted him in the face. Then, tossing the bottle aside, Ben turned to his players and wrapped his arms around those closest to him. When the boys quieted down, they turned to their coaches but continued to mess up one another's sweaty hair.

Ben grinned. "That was one of the most incredible games I've seen in my life. You guys deserve this win and the championship. You're Alberta champs."

"Yaaaaaaaay!" the boys shouted together, holding their index fingers high in the air.

"I'm proud of every one of you guys," Ben continued. "Now let's shake hands with Red Deer and get that trophy."

"Yaaaaaaaaa!" the boys yelled louder, then turned and ran to centre floor where the dejected Chiefs waited.

The Rams lined up and slowly moved forward, shaking hands with the Red Deer players. The odd player gave an opponent a tap on the head or a friendly slap on the shoulder, signs of respect for a battle well fought. As they finished, all the players on both teams lined up facing one another, waiting for the presentations that would end the tournament.

Moving to centre floor, a league official holding a microphone called for everyone's attention. Two other officials emerged through a side gate, holding the biggest trophy Mike had ever seen. He couldn't stop smiling, and once more bumped Ryan, who was standing beside him, and rubbed him hard on top of the head.

"Ladies and gentlemen, could I please have your attention?" The official paused as the crowd quieted down for the presentations. "Wasn't that one of the most incredible games you've ever seen?" The crowd yelled and clapped loudly. Smiling and holding up his hand, the official continued. "Games like this one show why lacrosse is the fastest growing sport in North America. And games like this one should make us all proud of our Alberta lacrosse players. Please join me in giving a talented bunch of boys from Red Deer who just wouldn't quit a huge round of applause."

The crowd cheered and was joined by the Rams on the floor. Despite the fact that they often thought they hated the Chiefs, the Rams knew that Red Deer had played its heart out.

"I would now ask the Chiefs' players to step forward to receive their silver medals as each player's name is called." Mike and the rest of the Rams stood politely but impatiently, applauding as each of their opponents came forward and received his medal.

"And now for the Alberta bantam lacrosse champions, the St. Albert Rams!"

The crowd went wild as the boys smiled from ear to ear and stepped forward to receive their gold medals. Some held their medal high in the air as they returned to the line of their teammates, while a couple jokingly bit down on the metal as if checking to see if the gold was real.

"I now ask," the official continued, "for Captains Ryan Domino, Mike Watson, and Spencer Lorenz to come forward to accept the Alberta Bantam Lacrosse Championship Trophy."

The Rams went crazy as Ryan, Mike, and Spencer walked to centre floor. The three boys held the trophy with league officials as pictures were taken. Then, grasping the trophy in both hands, Ryan hoisted it high above his head and cried, "We're number one!"

As soon as Ryan said that, the rest of the Rams rushed to centre floor, joining their captains. Each player took a turn gripping the trophy as the team slowly made its way around the arena. As they passed the trophy around, the players pumped it above their heads, almost dropping it more than once. Returning to centre floor, the Rams handed the trophy over to their coaches and grouped together for team pictures taken by excited parents who had entered the playing area. Mike, who was standing at the rear of the gathering, closed his eyes and tipped back his head. With a smile he thrust both his hands into the air, his index fingers raised as the sign for number one. This was unbelievable, he thought. And with most of the boys only thirteen now, next year could only be better. Mike himself would be fourteen.

CHAPTER 2

Last summer's championship seemed like a dream. What was happening now was more like a nightmare. Mike sat on his bed, his head in his hands, barely able to stop the tears welling in his eyes. Ryan, Cayln, and Spencer were leaning against the wall near the door to Mike's bedroom. No one really knew what to say.

"Mike, I don't … I mean …" Ryan stopped and shrugged as he helplessly looked at Cayln and Spencer.

"It sucks!" Cayln said forcefully.

Everyone, including Mike, looked up at Cayln, who was usually the quietest guy on the team. The anger in his voice had gotten everyone's attention. Cayln was forty-five kilograms soaking wet and normally silent and serious. He let his athleticism do the talking for him on the lacrosse floor, and when he did speak, it was to the point and softly. To hear such emotion in his voice and see the anger in his pale blue eyes surprised everyone.

"Well, it does," Cayln continued. "How can your dad do this? He has no right. I mean, can't you or your mom say something? It makes no sense. You can't just tell your family one day, 'Hey, guys, guess what? We're moving to the North Pole.' It really sucks!"

Mike shook his head. "It's not like that. Dad was transferred. Everybody in the RCMP gets transferred sooner or later."

"Yeah, but this busts apart our whole team," Spencer said. "We lose our coach. We lose our top scorer. We just lose. Cayln's right. The whole thing sucks." Spencer was one of the leaders on the team and wasn't afraid to speak his mind. He was big, and when he spoke or hit someone, it was with authority.

"Can't he tell his boss he won't go or something?" Ryan asked, wrinkling his nose. "I mean, they can't force him to go, can they?" Ryan was the joker in the crowd, and sometimes all Mike had to do was see the expression on his friend's freckled face to start laughing. But not today.

"I don't know ..." Mike mumbled. "I guess it means he gets a promotion if we move. If we don't move, he can stay here for a while, but then we still might have to move and he won't get promoted, or something like that."

"Do they even play lacrosse in Nunavuk or Inukituk or … whatever the place is you're going?" Spencer asked, exasperation apparent in his voice.

"It's Inuvik and it's in the Northwest Territories, Spencer," Mike said. "I don't know if they play lacrosse. I don't even know if they have a rink. I don't know anything about the place except it's somewhere inside the Arctic Circle and makes winter in St. Albert seem like summer."

Spencer shook his head. "Jeez, that does suck. Your dad wouldn't go there unless there was lacrosse, though, right? I mean, he loves lacrosse as much as us. I can't see him doing that."

Ryan groaned. "Maybe, since we won provincials, he wants to win a seal-hunting championship or something now."

Mike glanced up, and despite his mood, smiled. Ryan grinned, too, while Spencer began to chuckle. Then Cayln started to laugh, as well.

Still chuckling, Mike shook his head. "You know what really sucks? You guys won't be there. I won't know anybody. I've never had to move before. I won't know anybody and I'll likely have to try out all over again to make a team up there. I think the people up there are mostly First Nations. They're likely great at lacrosse, of course. They invented the game. Maybe I'll make their team and we'll come down here and kick your butts."

Ryan rolled his eyes. "Oh, yeah, right!"

"So do you guys leave as soon as summer holidays start?" Cayln asked.

"That's the other crappy part," Mike said. "I don't even get to finish school here. We move in early March."

"You can't be serious!" Spencer cried.

"That's just in two weeks!" Ryan added.

Mike gazed at the floor sadly. "I couldn't believe it, either. My mom's already started to pack. If you didn't notice, the garage is full of boxes. Get this. Apparently, there are two rivers you have to cross if you drive to Inuvik. In the winter the rivers are covered in ice. They freeze up and people drive over them. In the summer there are ferries. If we don't move now, then I guess once school is over is when the ice is melting on the rivers and they can't cross them for a while. That means they couldn't get trucks across with our stuff until all the ice is gone and the ferries are in the water. So we move now and they get the trucks over the ice with our stuff."

"I thought there was ice and snow up there all the time," Spencer said.

"No, only ten months out of twelve," a voice said behind the boys.

Turning quickly, they saw Ben Watson in the doorway in his RCMP uniform. He grinned when he saw the surprise on the boys' faces turn to dejection. Mike didn't even look up.

"I'm kidding. They actually have a great summer up there, and guess what? The sun never goes down. I'm not kidding about that part. They call it the midnight sun. The sun never goes down from late May to well into July."

"So are you guys going to drive up and go over that ice and stuff to get to Inuvik, too?" Ryan asked Ben.

"No, Ryan. The moving trucks will take our stuff up and over the Peel and Mackenzie Rivers. We'll fly up. It's a pretty long drive, and in winter the weather through the mountains in the Yukon can get pretty bad at times."

Spencer glanced at Mike. "I thought you guys were going to the Northwest Territories?"

"Inuvik's in the Northwest Territories," Ben said. "But to get there you have to drive up through northern B.C. and then across the Yukon. You go to Whitehorse and then on the Klondike Highway to Dawson City.

From there it can get a little hairy because you drive up through the mountains on the Dempster Highway to this place called Eagle Plains. Then you go down into the Northwest Territories. You cross the Peel River, go to a spot called Fort McPherson, and drive on to the Mackenzie River. Once you cross the Mackenzie, you go to Inuvik. That's it. The road doesn't go any farther. When you get to Inuvik, you have to fly if you're going farther north."

"Jeez!" Cayln blurted. "So, in other words, you're taking Mike to the end of the world."

Ben laughed. "Inuvik's actually the biggest community in the western Arctic."

"What exactly does *big* mean?" chimed in Spencer.

"Big means about thirty-five hundred people."

"And exactly how big is St. Albert?"

Ben frowned. "Well, about fifty thousand."

"O … kay," drawled Ryan. "So the Edmonton area's about a million people, St. Albert's about fifty thousand, and you're taking Mike to the bustling centre of the western Arctic where thirty-five hundred people live? Congratulations, Mike."

Mike smiled outwardly, but inside panic was starting to grip him.

"Listen, Ryan," Ben said, "you love hunting and fishing, right?"

Ryan nodded.

"Well, Inuvik's right on the Mackenzie River. In fact, it's in the Mackenzie Delta, which is one of the biggest deltas in the world. That means there are basically little rivers everywhere. Just to the north is the treeline. That means the tundra starts right there. To the southwest are the Richardson Mountains and the Yukon. There are lakes with some of the freshest water in the world all over the place. What does all that mean? It means no matter what direction you go, no matter what part of the river you take, you can go hunting for caribou, you can go fishing for trout or northern pike, you name it. There are moose, foxes, bald eagles all along the river. The place is incredible." Ben glanced around the room. Four faces with four blank stares stared right back at him. Shaking his head, he sighed.

"So, uh, Coach Watson," Ryan asked, "how much lacrosse exactly do they play in a place with thirty-five hundred people?"

Ben scratched his head. "Well … I was going to get to that. You see, the interesting thing is … well —"

"Ben!" a voice called from the hallway.

"Yes, honey?"

"I need you in the kitchen."

"Okay, boys, we can finish this later. Mike's mom needs me." Turning away, Ben exhaled noisily and headed down the hall, leaving the boys to wonder what he was going to say.

CHAPTER 3

Mike slumped against the wall of the plane and stared out the window at the runway in Edmonton. He couldn't really focus on anything in particular. Their final days in St. Albert had been a blur of boxes, handshakes, and goodbyes.

Cayln, Ryan, and Taylor had come to the airport to say goodbye. They had all stood around waiting for the flight to be called, shuffling their feet, not really knowing what to say. When the time came to go through security, Mike had glanced back. The image of his forlorn friends limply waving goodbye was still replaying in his mind.

Mike actually hadn't flown much before and on any other day would have been quite excited about this journey. Today, however, every time he started to pay attention to the details of the flight, his heart pulled him back into the sadness of what this trip really meant.

Somewhere in the foggy recesses of his brain, Mike heard the flight crew go over their spiel about how to fasten seat belts, the need to turn off all electronics, where the exits were, and what to do if oxygen masks dropped down in an emergency. Then the captain announced that their flight was next in line for take-off, and Mike shot a glance back at the terminal and wondered if Ryan, Cayln, and Taylor were watching from somewhere inside or if they were driving back to St. Albert. Driving home! Another wave of emotion swept over him as he realized he didn't even know what home looked like anymore.

Mike's attention reverted to the runway as the plane began to vibrate and the noise of the engines escalated to an almost uncomfortable level. Lurching forward, the plane hurtled along, gaining speed as the world Mike had grown up in rushed past with a blurry finality. Slowly, the front wheel lifted and the plane was completely off the ground, creating butter-flies in the pit of Mike's already unsettled stomach. He brooded as the ground fell away and the buildings of the surrounding area retreated into the distance. They began to circle away from Edmonton as their altitude increased, and Mike's last glimpse was the town of Leduc as it disappeared below the clouds.

After some time, they levelled off, and Mike felt the vibrations and sound of the plane settle into a consistent and steady drone. His ears were plugged, and he pinched his nose between his thumb and fore-finger and blew out air. Bubbles seemed to pop in each eardrum, and his hearing once again felt normal. Despondently, he focused on droplets of condensation that started to form on the outside window due to the altitude. The droplets took shape and grew in size until they became so plump that the wind drew them back in a stream that flowed along the window's edge and out of sight.

"What can I get you?" Mike's head snapped up as his mother tapped him on the shoulder. A flight attendant stood in the aisle and smiled at him as she motioned at the cart beside her. He opened his mouth to ask for a Pepsi, but the words got stuck in his throat.

"No thanks," he finally said as he turned back to the window, realizing at the same time that he actually was quite thirsty.

Jeannie smiled at the flight attendant. "He'll have a Pepsi." Reaching over with her left hand, she twisted the clasp that held Mike's table tray against the seat in front of him and lowered it, then placed a plastic cup of Pepsi and ice on the white surface.

After a moment or two, Mike glanced at the cup of Pepsi and then at his mother. She looked up from the magazine she was reading and smiled, then resumed reading. Mike picked up the cup of Pepsi, swirled the liquid a little, and watched as it fizzed and foamed. Then he brought the cup to his mouth and sipped. The Pepsi was cold, and when he swallowed, he enjoyed the icy tang as the carbonated liquid slipped down his throat.

His mother always knew what he really wanted, and for the first time he experienced a slight glimmer of hope, saw a tentative ray of light in the darkness. Mike got along great with his dad, but it was his mother who seemed to understand him best. She never failed to spot the small thread of positive in a whole blanket of negative. And every time she was right.

When he started lacrosse, he was six years old and was big for his age. Mike could hardly contain his excitement when his father informed him he was registered in lacrosse, and had begged to go to the rink to watch the game he would soon play. He badgered his father non-stop on the way there with questions about the rules and who would be on his team. When they arrived at the rink, he jumped from the car as soon as they parked and despite warning yells from his dad ran ahead and through the doors. Weaving his way through the crowd of adults, he unwittingly ended up at one of the indoor fields in the huge complex where midget-age players were being evaluated for placement on teams. His mouth dropped open as he stood and watched the players beat one another with their sticks, violently trying to impress the evaluators. As his father approached, he turned, tears streaming down his face, and ran right back out to the car, terrified that the same thing was going to happen to him.

Eventually, Ben managed to drag him to the rink, and he began to enjoy the game, playing with other boys his age. But he was terrible. Every time he ran he tripped and fell. He couldn't catch and never remembered to cradle the ball in his stick. It was his mother who held him when he cried after his first game, reassuring him that one day he would be the best player on the floor. She was also the one who practised with him every day when his father was on shift. Jeannie was a short, dark, wiry woman who enjoyed all athletics and loved seeing her son develop a passion for sports as he grew up. It hadn't happened immediately, but bit by bit Mike improved until by the end of the season he was, in fact, the best on his team.

When his father announced they were moving north, once again it was his mother who kept telling him that everything would be all right. Every day she would say some new fact about Inuvik or about the North. And every day Mike would shake his head and get more depressed. Now for the first time he realized that his mother might be right.

Raising the cup of Pepsi to his lips, Mike took another sip and returned his gaze to the window. The clouds were now intermittent, and the land below was beginning to change. North of Edmonton the patch-work quilt of farmland spread to the horizon, and a criss-cross of roads of various sizes sliced through the pattern. The farther north they travelled the more forest areas intruded on the land that had been cleared to grow crops, with only the odd road disturbing the rural mosaic.

Now the ground was quite different. Without Mike noticing, it had shifted from a patchwork pattern to a pockmarked array of lakes, ponds, rivers, and what appeared to be marshes. And there was snow! It was early March and an unexpected thaw had melted all of the snow in the Edmonton/St. Albert area. But not here. The lakes were still frozen, and the wooded areas were full of snow. With every kilometre they covered it seemed to get whiter, causing Mike's brief interlude of positive thinking to evaporate.

* * *

There wasn't much to see in Yellowknife. The stop was brief, and they were in the terminal for a short time. The terminal was nice, but Mike figured about forty buildings that size could be fitted into the terminal in Edmonton. It was located outside Yellowknife, so all they saw were the surrounding airport hangars, warehouses, scrubby trees, and snow. Lots of snow.

The flight from Edmonton to Yellowknife had taken about an hour and forty minutes, and it was another hour and a half to Inuvik. If there was this much snow in Yellowknife, what was waiting farther north?

When they took off from Yellowknife, Mike had a brief view of the city — a few taller buildings and lots of rock and snow. As they flew northwest toward Inuvik, it seemed all he saw was frozen water, stunted trees, snow, and ... more rock. He had never seen anything like it. It was as if they were flying over the moon and its craters were full of frozen water. His eyes began to feel heavy, and before he understood what was happening, he nodded off to sleep.

Mike wasn't sure if his mother had nudged him or if he had woken up on his own. Sleepily, he sat up and rubbed his mouth with the back of his hand. He had been sleeping with his head against the hard wall of the plane, and his neck was stiff and sore as he swiv-elled, trying to rid himself of the knots in his muscles. Then he noticed his mother smiling at him.

She pointed at the window. "We're landing."

Craning his head, Mike took a look. "How long was I asleep?"

Jeannie studied her watch. "I'm guessing about forty-five minutes. It's three-thirty. Why?"

Mike pressed his face against the window. "It's gloomy outside, but it's three-thirty in the afternoon."

"It's early March and we're inside the Arctic Circle," his mother said.

"So?"

"So they lose the sun in the winter and it still isn't very intense yet."

Mike darted a look at his father. "They lose the sun?"

Ben nodded. "Your mother's right. They lose the sun."

"Well, when do they find it?" Mike asked dreamily.

"*Pffffffft!*" Ben burst into laughter, then covered his mouth and quickly turned away to face the aisle.

Jeannie swatted her husband. "Ben! The boy's ask-ing a perfectly good question. Don't pay any attention to him, Mike. Losing the sun is a figure of speech. What I meant was that we're so far north that there's a period of time in the winter when the sun stays below the horizon: I think it happens in December and January. Then it starts to get twilight and the sun comes back above the horizon. It gets light in the morning and afternoon this time of year, but not as strongly as it does once summer comes."

Mike glanced out the window again.

"Can you see anything, honey?" Jeannie asked.

It was snowing. Big, fluffy flakes swirled in the air outside the plane, making visibility almost impossible. Mike pressed his face as close to the window as he could and squinted, focusing on the ground below, but the utter whiteness of the world outside made his eyes sting. As the plane continued to lose altitude, the land started to take shape — more frozen lakes, more dwarf trees, more rocks, and more snow, a lot more snow.

"This is so exciting!" his mother gushed, gripping his arm and looking over her son's shoulder. "What can you see, Mike?"

"Well, Mom, I see this white stuff floating in the air. And I see this white stuff all over the ground. Oh, wait a second. Yeah, I was right. I see white stuff all around a lake that has this frozen stuff covering the surface."

"Oh, stop it!" she said, feigning a light slap on his arm. "I bet that white stuff is full of snowmobile trails just waiting for you and your dad to explore."

Mike stared at his mother, a puzzled expression creasing the bridge of his nose. "But we don't have a —" He stopped speaking when he noticed his mother's smile broaden. Leaning forward, he glanced at his father, who nodded. "You mean we have a … a …"

Ben laughed. "We have *two* snowmobiles."

"Holy crap!" Mike cried. "I thought you said you hated snowmobiling. Didn't you say it's a lazy man's hobby and that only guys with big bellies who are too lazy to ski or skate and who love to drink litres of beer on the weekend like to skidoo?"

"This is different, Mike," Ben said. "It's not like a southern hobby here. We can snowmobile from our back door into the bush and take our pick of trails to hunt or just explore and watch caribou and other animals. And in the summer we can jump into our boat on the Mackenzie River and find some new channel to explore every time we go out."

Mike couldn't contain himself. "Oh, my God. We don't have two —"

"No, we'll only have one boat, but it's a pretty nice second-hand speedboat that I got from one of the other RCMP officers in Inuvik."

Mike grinned. Maybe, just maybe, this was going to be the adventure his father had promised.

CHAPTER 4

The thud of the plane making contact with the runway and the force of the brakes as the plane quickly decelerated forced Mike back into his seat, his head sinking into the cushion. A fine cloud of snow created by the jet engines blew up around the windows, highlighted by the brightness of the landing lights as the plane slowed down and prepared to taxi to the terminal. With the cabin lights dimmed, once the snow settled outside the plane Mike got a better view of his surroundings.

There was a slight, pinkish-orange band of light across the sky. The light around the band of colour was powder blue, which wasn't quite right as a description, though. Mike had trouble putting his finger on what was so different about the hue. He had never seen anything like its soft, misty, textured look. "Out of this world" came to mind. And given the fact they had just landed in Inuvik, Mike figured that might not be far off.

If the terminal in Yellowknife was forty times smaller than the one in Edmonton, then this one was at least eighty times smaller. Mike watched as an airport worker swung two illuminated orange wands back and forth over his shoulders, directing the plane toward the building. He strained his neck, trying to see the front of the plane. The terminal was a single-storey, two-tone brown building, and he wasn't sure what kind of a tunnel they would use to walk from the plane inside. The airport worker stopped swinging his wands and crossed them above his head. The plane lurched to a stop without a tunnel in sight.

Mike blinked as the cabin lights flashed on. The sound of metal clacked throughout the plane as people hurriedly undid their seat belts, jumped up, and anxiously pulled carry-on luggage from the overhead bins. Mike watched as his father stepped into the aisle and stretched to full height. Reaching into the overhead bin, he pulled down a duffle bag that Mike had barely noticed when they boarded the flight. Ben zipped open the bag and methodically pulled out three dark blue parkas with fur-trimmed hoods. He unfolded each one and fluffed them into full size and shape.

After dropping one into Jeannie's lap, he passed one over to Mike.

"You've got to be kidding," Mike said, snorting. "I don't need this. It gets real cold in St. Albert in the winter, and I've never worn one of these." Before his father could answer, a clank and hiss pulled Mike's attention to the front of the plane.

One of the flight attendants had unlocked the front door and was now swinging it open. A blast of frigid air and fog blew through the opening and filled the front of the cabin. The attendant's face instantly turned pink, and she threw her hood up to cover her head. A few seconds later the cold hit Mike where he sat by the window. Lowering his gaze, he silently pulled the parka over his jacket and zipped it up.

Mike followed his parents to the front of the plane and stepped out the door. A gale struck his face and momentarily sucked the breath from his body. He gulped and gasped before he was able to breathe properly again. As he walked down the stairs that extended from the side of the plane, the cold pierced his jeans. When he exhaled, each breath hung in the air like a cloud of smoke before it was swirled away by the wind. The cold stung his ears, and he quickly pulled up the parka's hood and held it against his cheek.

Walking close behind his parents, Mike quickly

hopped up the steps of the terminal and pushed through the doors to the welcoming warmth inside. Flipping down his hood, he put the palms of his hands against his cheeks and felt the cold drawing away from his skin. In the terminal people stood in small groups, smiling and excitedly speaking to loved ones and friends. When Mike gazed at the room full of unfamiliar faces, a surge of homesickness swamped him.

"Sergeant Watson!" Mike glanced up and spotted the owner of the voice. A thin, red-haired man in an RCMP parka and dark blue uniform pants with the familiar yellow stripes down the sides approached through the crowd.

"He means you," Jeannie whispered in Ben's ear, lightly tugging at his parka.

"I know he means me," Ben said, slightly stooping as he waved and held the man's gaze.

Jeannie giggled. "I know. It just sounds so nice after all these years."

The move to Inuvik had been contingent on a promotion for Ben from corporal to sergeant. Ben had done his time, and it felt good.

"Corporal Thomas Fitzgerald, sir," the man said, extending a hand.

Fitzgerald was tall but slightly shorter than Ben and lighter in build. He appeared to be in his early thirties, which would make him a bit younger than Mike's father. His hair was wiry and cropped so close to his scalp that it almost seemed painted on, like that of a GI Joe Mike had played with when he was younger.

Ben shook the man's hand firmly. "Call me Ben."

The corporal grinned. "They call me Fitz."

Ben turned to his family. "This is my wife, Jeannie, and my son, Mike."

Fitz smiled warmly and shook Jeannie's hand first, then Mike's. "Nice grip, son." He turned to Ben. "Big boy. He's going to be a hot ticket for hockey here."

"I play lacrosse," Mike blurted.

Fitz looked blankly at Mike. "Well, Mike, I don't know about that. I guess you might have to play hockey here."

"How's the snowmobiling been?" Ben cut in.

"Just incredible," Fitz said. "Believe it or not, we usually don't get a lot of snow here in the winter. It drops to about minus twenty and stays there pretty much all season long. Of course, we get plenty of snow to skidoo, but not buckets like most people from the south think. It pretty much stays too cold for a lot of snow. We get spells where it's minus thirty and colder, but in the last week we've been getting what you see outside." He waved at the terminal window. "The weather warms up, we get a storm with a dump of snow, and then it cools off again. With the day-light coming back so quickly now, it's just fantastic. Lots of snow, about ten hours of daylight and getting brighter, and for the most part around minus fifteen to minus twenty. You'll find quite a few people going out to camps and getting caribou right now with the warmer weather. Most people will stay in town today, but when things clear up tomorrow or the next day the town will be a bit deserted."

"That sounds fantastic," Jeannie said, placing her arm around Mike's shoulder and squeezing.

It did sound great to Mike, and he momentarily forgot what Fitz might have meant with his comments about hockey.

"Here come the bags, guys." Fitz motioned toward the carousel behind them. "What are we looking for?" They all headed over and pointed out the suitcases as they came through an opening in the side of the building. The Watsons had six altogether. It would be a week before the moving truck arrived in Inuvik, so they had taken as much with them as possible.

Once everything was located, it was back into the cold. They hurriedly tossed the luggage into the rear of the RCMP Explorer and clambered inside, shutting out the wind and blowing snow. Mike sat in back with his mother, while Ben took a seat up front with Fitz.

Drawing back his hood, Mike shivered as the hot air in the idling vehicle closed around him. When he pushed his hands against his thighs, he swore he could feel the cold rising out of the skin.

Fitz nosed the Explorer out of its parking spot and headed away from the airport. "If we turned right, the road would take us to the Mackenzie River ferry crossing. You can take the ferry over to Tsiigehtchic, or to the main landing where the highway goes to Fort McPherson and then through the mountains to the Yukon. Beautiful drive, but it can beat the heck out of your vehicle."

"How far is it into town?" Jeannie asked.

"About fourteen kilometres," Fitz said, looking at her in the rearview mirror. "Over to the left is a pretty nice campground in the summer. There's a tower that gives a great view of the delta. The weather looks pretty harsh out there right now, but it's a beautiful place. I don't know what it is, but people seem to either love it or hate it. You hear stories all the time about folks who plan to work up here for a couple of years and spend twenty. Then there's the other side of things where people head here with a northern dream and leave after a couple of months because they hate it."

Mike glanced at Fitz's face in the mirror. Their eyes briefly met, and the corporal's smile took on an unsettling menace, bathed in green from the glow of the dashboard. Mike quickly shifted his concentration back to the road. He wondered which kind of people they would be. Would they love Inuvik or hate it? He shivered again as another ripple of cold seemed to flow out of his body. Right now he had to admit his vote would be pretty strong on the hate side of things. Narrowing his eyes, he stared at the red taillights of other vehicles ahead of them. This time, however, he spotted some white lights.

"Welcome to Inuvik," Fitz said, waving at some buildings on their right. "That's the Finto Inn, and over there's the Nova Inn where you folks will be staying." They drove up a small hill and continued into town. "We're on Mackenzie Road, which is the main street. It goes right through Inuvik."

Ben pointed to the left. "Is that the hospital?"

Fitz nodded. "It sure is. To the right is all residential. Our newer homes are mostly to the right, and they continue up over what's called Co-op Hill. There are quite a few older homes down toward the river. We're almost downtown. Wouldn't you know it? Our one traffic light and your first time here it's going to be red."

Mike watched as the light shifted from orange to red. "Did you say your *one* light?"

All three adults turned and looked at Mike's puzzled face.

"I sure did," Fitz said. "This is our one and only traffic light whether we need it or not. Apparently, well before my time, a group of exchange students came up here from southern Canada. They were so excited about their visit that they wanted to give the town something to remember them by. Something we didn't have. Well, this is it — our one and only traffic light."

"Holy crap!" Mike said.

"To the left is the post office," Fitz said. "Past that are the RCMP station and your house. We'll go there after. Over to the right are the schools. Mike, you'll go to that one." He pointed. "Samuel Hearne Secondary School. It has grades seven through twelve. Behind the other school you can see the Inuvik Family Centre. It has an arena, a curling rink, and a fitness centre. The conference centre there has a pool, squash courts, and a play zone for kids."

Mike strained to see the schools and the complex behind them.

"Light's green." Fitz shifted the Explorer ahead. "To the right is one of the big tourist attractions in Inuvik. The Igloo Church is a pretty distinctive landmark, for sure. You know, Mike, they say they built it that way so the devil can never corner you."

49

Mike smiled weakly at Fitz's lame joke. He had to admit the building looked pretty cool. It was brilliantly lit, and sure enough, it was in the shape of an igloo. The building was round, and of course white. A set of wide stairs led to the front double doors, which boasted elaborate stained glass windows. A blue cross extended from the roof of the entranceway. The dome of the church was silver and shone brightly in the surrounding darkness. On top of the dome sat another circular structure with tall, narrow stained glass windows completely around the outside. On the very top was a tall blue cross. Mike sat back. *Okay*, he thought, *so people don't live in igloos here, but they go to church in them.*

They drove on slowly, Fitz giving them time to glance in every direction as they proceeded. "It's going to look a lot different tomorrow when the weather clears up, but this gives you the lay of the land."

"The population is thirty-five hundred?" Jeannie asked the corporal.

Fitz nodded. "That's pretty much bang on. I think the last count was thirty-five hundred and twenty or something."

Mike paid attention with part of his brain, but the other part started to drift off. He slumped in his seat and dreamily listened to the adults continue to talk, his head propped against the back of the seat and window.

"On the right is our Northern Store," Fitz said. "It carries everything from groceries and clothes to hardware. They do pretty well getting in fresh food. Of course, things get more expensive and a bit dicey when the ferry's out in the fall and the ice road's breaking up in spring."

"Fitz, you said that like it's the only store in town," Jeannie said. "Where else do people shop?"

"Well, Jeannie, the Northern Store's pretty much it for groceries and clothing of any variety. Quite a few people drive over to Whitehorse from time to time to get stuff you can't pick up here, but the Northern Store has pretty much all the necessities."

Mike's mother sat back to ponder this information. "One main store," she murmured. "My, my, my."

Ben half turned and smiled at his wife. "Look on the bright side, Jeannie. We live less than a minute from *the* store. We can skip over, shop for what we need, and be home in a flash. Pretty great, eh?"

Jeannie shook her head. "You're such a *man*!"

Fitz chuckled. "You'll get used to it. I bet every husband and wife who moves here have had this conversation. It just makes trips to Yellowknife, Edmonton, and Whitehorse all the more special. Quite a few of the wives do a tonne of mail order, too. Get out those catalogues."

51

Ben groaned. "I don't think you're helping, Fitz."

Mike's head fell back heavier into the corner of the window and seat, his mind fogging over with sleep. His face felt warmer and warmer. He was barely aware of the droning voices around him, and the movement of the vehicle lulled him deeper into slumber.

The next thing he knew he was blinking. Not sure of his surroundings, he opened his eyes wide. His mother had her hand on his shoulder and was pointing out the window on his side of the Explorer.

"Look, Mike, our new house," she said.

He shifted his gaze out the window and followed the direction of her finger.

"It's so cute," she added.

It might have been cute, but it was small. It looked like an A-frame and had a very steeply pitched roof.

"They're not big, but they're cozy," Fitz said. "Great location and close to work and to Mike's school. Pretty much close to everything in town."

"We were close to everything even when we were at the airport," Mike said groggily.

"Well, it's home, Mike," Ben said. "When you were taking your nap, Fitz had some exciting news, too. The moving truck actually got here yesterday. Our stuff's inside the house. We'll stay at the hotel tonight, but we can move in tomorrow. Everything will seem a little better when you get into your own bedroom and unpack your own things."

"My bedroom's in St. Albert," Mike muttered, turning back to the window.

He slid down in the seat and closed his eyes. What would the kids be like in Inuvik? He was good-natured and made friends easily. His mother was of South African descent, and the mixture of features she had passed on to him often made it difficult for people to place him. With his large, expressive, dark brown eyes, caramel skin, and loosely curled black hair, he usually fitted in no matter where he went. People guessed he was everything from Dene and East Asian to East Indian and African Canadian.

Although short for his age at fourteen, he was built like a muscular bowling ball: wide shoulders, thick chest, and massive legs and butt. Whether it was for hockey, lacrosse, or any other contact sport, he always surprised his opposition. If they hadn't played against him before and saw him in equipment for the first time, they had no idea that he likely outweighed them by a good ten kilograms and was one of the fastest, most competitive players they would face.

But what if none of that mattered to anyone in Inuvik? What would he do?

CHAPTER 5

Fitz was wrong. Inuvik didn't look that much different the next day. After an early breakfast at the hotel, Fitz had picked them up and taken them to the house. Mike recognized Mackenzie Road from the previous night: hospital, stop at *the* light, post office, turn left, police station, house. The A-frame appeared even smaller in the mid-morning sunlight.

Mike had to admit that though the town appeared the same, the weather was a whole lot better. The sun shone brightly and reflected off the snow, making him squint as he stepped down from the Explorer. Tiny crystals in the snow glistened like millions of diamonds. They were in the air, too, and made him feel disoriented as he blinked, momentarily snow-blinded. Fitz said they were ice crystals. Even though it was sunny, the air temperature had dropped to minus thirty-five, which was unseasonably cold, Fitz told them. Unseasonably cold! Did they even have other seasons up here?

The big winter boots his father had given him that morning crunched loudly on the snow. He stopped in the driveway and took in his new neighbourhood through the frozen mist of his breath. Most of the buildings seemed pretty old. The police station was next to their house, and other than the post office and the schools he could see across Mackenzie Road, he didn't know what anything else was. As his eyes adjusted to the brightness, he did notice one thing. Because the snow was so white, the colours of the buildings were incredibly bright. Even the brown of their house was intense. *Jeez, get a grip, Mike*, he thought, shaking his head.

"Mike, let's go inside," his mother said.

He followed his parents and Fitz toward the house he was supposed to call home.

"This door at the side is basically your front door," Fitz said. "Let's go around to the back door, though, because it'll give you a view of the yard and I can show you through from there."

They followed a wooden walkway along the side of the house, then turned right at the back and came to the other entrance. Absent-mindedly, Mike glanced around the yard as Fitz fumbled with the key. It wasn't a bad-sized space — bigger than his yard back in St. Albert at least. Lots of snow and a few scraggly trees. Mike's attention was drawn to a long, rectangular tube covered with corrugated metal. Running along the back of their lot, it continued in both directions out of sight and stood off the ground on thick wooden logs spaced at intervals. The logs held the tube about a metre off the ground. The tube itself was about a metre high and perhaps a metre across. A section branched off and entered their yard, disappearing into the side of the house. As Mike scanned both directions, he saw where the tube branched off into other buildings in the area.

"There we go," Fitz said, pushing open the door. "Let's head inside."

Mike followed the others inside. The smell of fresh paint, Mr. Clean, and stale air assailed his nostrils simultaneously.

"It's freshly painted, and we had a couple of ladies come in and clean things from top to bottom," said Fitz, struggling to kick off his heavy boots. "To be quite honest, Jeannie, Sergeant MacLean's wife, Gwen, was awfully fussy, so it was pretty clean to begin with. This is the storage room, and the crawl space is right under here." Fitz lifted a piece of the floor by a metal ring fixed in the centre. "If you bring in a barge order, this is where you can store most of your supplies. Seems a bit odd, since we have a road up from the South and so on, but it can save you a heap of money."

The house was built on wooden supports like the ones holding up the metal tube in the backyard. Mike noticed a miniature bathroom to his left as he walked ahead into the kitchen. There was a table and chairs, and he remembered for the first time that the house was owned by the RCMP and came with its own furniture. Their furniture was stored back in St. Albert. There were boxes with KITCHEN scrawled across them along one wall. That would be the stuff the movers had dropped off.

The kitchen was small, too. As he moved ahead, he realized the whole house was tiny, and pretty plain, as well. The walls were off-white. The floor in the kitchen was white linoleum with a checkered black pattern. He passed through the kitchen into a living room with a dining area to the right. The floor had a nondescript dark brown carpet, and judging by the drag marks, it had been recently shampooed. To the left was a set of stairs. Beyond that was a small room that could be used as a study or bedroom. Mike heard voices above him and started up the stairs, which were steep and covered in dark brown carpet. That made him realize how pointed the roof of the house was, and he wondered what the bedrooms looked like.

There was a bathroom at the top of the stairs, and a hallway extended to his left and right. The same nauseating brown carpet flowed out of sight in both directions like a muddy river without an end. He turned left, away from the voices, and wandered into what had to be a bedroom. Judging by the twin bed against one wall, this was his room.

The walls to his left and right rose more than a metre. At that point the ceiling angled up to a peak in the middle. The walls were off-white and the carpet was the same dirty brown. There was a window on the far side of the room. Mike wandered over and stared into the backyard. He could now see over the metal tube. Trees and other houses sat silently on hidden streets. In the distance he thought he spied a lake, but with the snow and brightness outside, it was hard to tell. Mike moved away from the window and allowed himself to sink into a sitting position on the bed. It felt soft. Too soft.

Glancing around, he spotted two identical dark brown wooden dressers. Each drawer had two silly-looking metal handles. A hard wooden chair sat just inside the room's door. Several piles of boxes were stacked against the far wall. These were marked: BOY'S ROOM. Those were his things. They didn't belong here. They belonged thousands of kilometres away in St. Albert.

"I see you found it on your own," Jeannie said.

Mike looked up to see Fitz and his parents standing in the doorway. They all had a goofy "Well, what do you think?" expression on their faces. He managed a weak smile and gazed out the window again.

"Well, I won't impose on you folks any longer," Fitz said, "because I bet you're anxious to unpack. If you can't find anything, just let me know, Ben. You know where to find me." He motioned in the direction of the police station.

The adults moved away and headed back downstairs. Waiting for a moment or two until the voices were nothing more than a murmur, Mike buried his face in his hands and began to cry.

CHAPTER 6

God, I don't want to go to school, Mike thought. He stood on the back porch, gripped the wooden railing through his ski gloves, and rocked back and forth as he stared at the backyard. Stopping, he pursed his lips and blew a visible stream of breath into the air like a jet. What a stupid place! Minus twenty something in early March. Loads of snow. And what was that metal thing in the backyard, anyway? It looked dumb out there. Despite the cold, he felt the warmth of anger rise in his face and began to shake his head. He was mad at a big metal thing that couldn't even return his anger. How sad was that?

"It's a utilidoor."

The voice wasn't loud, and it took Mike a few seconds to realize someone had spoken. He straightened and searched around. To his left he spotted a man leaning on an ice scraper in the police station parking lot. The brightening sky outlined the stranger's silhouette against the buildings but made it impossible to see his features because the backlight threw shadows across his face.

"It has pipes in it," the man continued. "There's too much permafrost here to bury them. They run all around behind the houses and take the water in and out. If they were in the ground, the permafrost would snap them like twigs and nothing would work."

Mike didn't know what to say, so he just nodded.

"I'm Victor Allen."

Mike nodded again. The man wore a dark blue parka, but not like the one his father had given him. This one was made of a softer homemade material with dark fur around the hood. Real fur. The man wore a baseball cap, and by the slight glint Mike detected when the stranger moved his head, he had to be wearing glasses. Mike was pretty sure the fellow was aboriginal, but he could never get the names right. There were Dene people and Inuvalut, or something like that. The guys who used to be called Eskimos.

"You don't have a name?" Victor Allen asked.

The man smiled, and Mike couldn't help but smile back. "I'm Mike Watson."

"*Qanaqitpit*, Mike Watson. That means 'how are you' in our Inuvialuit language."

Inuvialuit! That was it. The people who lived in the Northwest Territories who used to be called Eskimos were Inuvialuit. The people in Nunavut who used to be called Eskimos were called Inuit. It was like a social studies lesson right outside his house. It felt funny to even think that. *His house.*

"Now this is where you would say '*Nakuurunga*, Victor.'"

"*Nagarunka*, Mr. Allen," Mike said.

Victor winced. "That's close enough, Mike. You must be the new RCMP sergeant's son. Welcome to Inuvik."

"Thank you, Mr. Allen." It wasn't a very imaginative thing to say back, but that was all Mike could muster.

"Now if I was a young guy like you, I'd hustle off to school, because I'm guessing within the next five minutes or so you're going to be late."

School! Mike rushed down the porch steps and up the wooden walkway to the street. "See you, Mr. Allen!" he called over his shoulder.

"See you, Mike."

Mike dashed past the post office and slowed down as he approached Mackenzie Road at the light. It was red! And the orange hand was flashing. One light in town half a block away from their house, and every time he'd been there it was red. He looked both ways and without stopping ran across the street. If he had tried that in St. Albert this time of the morning, he would have died a quick and painful death. As it was, a truck approached the intersection after he crossed. The driver beeped his horn and waved as he passed by.

His feet were heavy in his winter boots, and despite the cold he started to sweat under his toque and parka. He slowed to a walk as he neared the school, noticing other students casually strolling up to the doors. Everything still seemed so much like a dream. No waking up extra early. No walking to the bus stop. No twenty-minute bus ride across town to school. Hat on, parka on, boots on, out the door, hike a block, cross a road at *the* light, take a few more steps, enter school. Welcome to the Outer Limits!

The school didn't look like much. As with every other building he'd seen in Inuvik, it was elevated on piles. There were two distinct parts or buildings joined by a short walkway with doors in the middle. The exterior was clad in aluminum siding that was a combination of faded yellow and tan. Looking quite out of place with the otherwise drab exterior was a bright red trim that ran around the top of the structure. The thought that maybe the builders had run out of tan-and-yellow material as they finished the school occurred to Mike. The part to the right of the walkway had two storeys, and the part to the left had SAMUEL HEARNE SECONDARY SCHOOL displayed in big letters across the front.

As Mike approached the front doors, he paid closer attention to the other students, which caused his stomach to lurch. Nobody else was dressed in heavy winter clothing. Ski jackets, snowboarding coats, ball caps or no hats, and running shoes or moccasin-like footwear were apparent everywhere. Mike halted just outside the doors and studied his heavy white winter boots.

"Nice moon boots," a girl commented as she pushed by and in through the doors.

Any thought Mike had of fleeing home was shattered when a loud buzzer sounded just above the doors in front of him. Other students shoved by, and he realized he was getting more than his share of dirty looks for blocking easy access to both doors. Pulling himself together, he kick-started his legs and waded inside.

Tentatively, Mike edged a few paces into the school, then stopped to get his bearings. The air was overpoweringly warm against his face as he pulled the toque off his head. There was a mixture of smells: warm bodies, sweat, floor wax, musty paper, and a smoky, somewhat pleasant aroma that Mike guessed was caused by the moccasin-like footwear and fur mittens some of the students wore.

"You look a little lost and a little South."

Mike sensed a hand on his shoulder. Turning, he glimpsed the smiling face of a lady who he figured was one of the teachers. She was tall with closely cropped grey hair — business-looking but not too severe.

"This is my first day," Mike said.

"Well, follow me." The teacher motioned, stepping ahead in quick, purposeful fashion without glancing back. "The office is this way. They'll get you all set up and headed to the right homeroom."

Mike followed, his boots squeaking on the shiny tile floor, which was quite wet in places from the morning traffic of students coming in from the snow. Everything looked pretty much the same as in any school. The halls were narrow and lined with lockers set into the wall. Most of the lockers were tan, but there was the odd red or black one that seemed to have been added as an afterthought. The ceiling was white tile stuff, and the walls were off-white or brown panel in some places. The floor in every direction was brown tile.

After a quick stop in the office where they seemed to be expecting him, one of the staff led him to an orange locker where he thankfully deposited his toque, mitts, heavy parka, and moon boots, replacing the last with the running shoes he'd stored in his backpack.

When he entered his homeroom class, he was relieved to see he was now pretty much dressed the same as everyone else — jeans, T-shirt, and running shoes. A few kids sported the high-top moccasin things he'd seen earlier. He would have to find out what they were because they looked pretty comfortable.

His homeroom teacher, Ms. Delorme, didn't make him stand up but welcomed him and told everyone his name and where he was from. She was a kindly lady with a smile that never seemed to leave her face. Not much taller than Mike, she was plump but not rotund. With greying brown hair and expressive, almost black eyes, she appeared matronly, but there was no doubt she was in charge. Ms. Delorme was one of those teachers who viewed each student as part of her brood and woe to whoever interfered with any of her charges.

She went on to mention who Mike's father was, which made him feel uncomfortable. He couldn't tell whether the heat in his cheeks was from the warmth of the school after being cold outside or from blood surging to the surface from embarrassment. Planting herself at the front of the class, Ms. Delorme breezed through a review of the previous day's English lesson. Not having been part of the prior discussions, Mike slumped in his seat and tried not to be conspicuous as he surveyed the students around him.

It was pretty much a sea of brown faces. There were two or three students who were obviously white, but everyone else was either Inuvialuit or Dene. Some looked a little more his colour, and he guessed they were a mix like him, Métis perhaps or a combination of Inuvialuit and white. His new situation seemed weird, and the irony wasn't lost on him.

St. Albert was pretty "white bread." There weren't many visible minorities. In fact, all of the guys he knew in school there were white as white could be. Every guy he played lacrosse with was, too. Mike had been the only boy of mixed parentage. But he had never felt out of place. Now he sat in a class brimming with brown kids his own age and some youths exactly the same colour as he was, yet he felt like an alien who didn't belong. Pretty weird.

Mike was sitting by the door and guessed there were about thirty students in total. The class itself was big but much the same as any he'd been in: shiny brown tile floor, off-white walls, a blackboard, the teacher's desk at the front, whiteboards at the sides, geography posters from around the world, and orange, yellow, and blue handmade posters with pictures depicting various Shakespearean and other literary themes.

The desks were rectangular metal ones — smooth shiny top, compartment inside, and four legs. The compartment in this kind of desk always scared the heck out of Mike. You couldn't see all the way to the back and never knew what was or had been in there. The kid before you might have been a nose-picker, and who knew where he'd wiped or flicked his sticky treasure. There was always gooey, stuck-on gum underneath such desks, too.

"Let's get started, Mike."

Mike glanced up to see Ms Delorme smiling pleasantly at him.

"While everyone else is reading, move your chair up to my desk and we'll see where you're at. Your marks from St. Albert are quite good, so I don't anticipate you'll have any problem jumping right in with the class."

Feeling the flush of embarrassment fill his cheeks once more, Mike sheepishly dragged his chair away from his desk and placed it beside Ms. Delorme. He looked back at the rest of the class and saw a few students staring at him before they returned their attention to the books in front of them. How much worse could this get? New kid in town. Dad a cop. New kid in class. New kid sitting with the teacher alone at the front of the class. Wonderful!

Ms. Delorme went through the materials the class had covered to date. Much to Mike's relief it was largely the same stuff he'd been working on in St. Albert. Ms. Delorme was helpful and did her best to make Mike feel at ease, but he started to squirm, imagining the eyes of the other students on the back of his head. It was with welcome relief that he lurched to his feet when the bell rang to end the first period.

Scrambling back to his desk, he gathered his books and almost sprinted to the door, lowering his head and trying not to meet the scrutiny of the other students. Without looking up, he dodged out the door, quickly turned right, and barrelled down the hall. It was too late when he spotted a huge pair of feet planted firmly in front of him. Unable to stop, he ran headlong into what felt like a brick wall. The force of contact popped the books out of his hands, scattering them in every direction as he stumbled backward and landed on his back.

Laughter echoed down the hall. It took a few seconds before Mike was able to push himself onto his elbows. Standing over him was the biggest kid he'd ever seen. Rolling forward onto his hands and knees, Mike got into a crouch and staggered upright into a standing position. The boy towering over him glowered and slowly clenched and unclenched his fists.

"Jeez, I'm sorry," Mike mumbled. Glancing around, he realized the hall was almost deserted. Everyone seemed to have run for cover with the exception of a couple of students who appeared ready to flee at any moment. Turning back to the boy, Mike had no idea what to do. The kid was close to two metres tall, with broad shoulders and an athletic build. His jet-black hair and dark brown skin accentuated the total blackness of his eyes. He had the hint of a scar on his left cheek that made the tightness of his mouth all the more threatening.

There was no backing down. There were no teachers in the hall, and something told Mike no one else was going to step in. He tensed his body and slowly raised his hands boxing-style, level with his chin.

Mike wasn't sure, but he thought he saw something change in the boy's expression — something small and almost imperceptible, but something nevertheless. The boy shook his head, then without warning ploughed Mike out of the way and moved past. Realizing he'd been holding his breath, Mike exhaled and sagged as the big kid sailed by. Almost afraid to look, he turned, anyway, and watched the big bruiser saunter down the hall. When the kid reached the far end, he stopped. Pausing, he fired a long, hard look at Mike, who shivered as those dark eyes that seemed so full of hate pierced him. Quickly spinning on his heel, the boy drew back and punched the last locker with all his might. The resounding crash made Mike jump as it echoed through the almost empty hall. Then, turning the corner, the huge kid was gone.

The few students who had witnessed the whole affair were still gazing at Mike as if anticipating some sort of mental breakdown or freak-out. Certain he was shaking, Mike squatted and began to gather the books and papers scattered across the tiles. "Jeez, why do they have grade twelves in the same school as us?" he muttered to himself. "I hate 'em!"

"He just turned fourteen and he's in grade nine," a harsh female voice said directly above him.

Snapping his head up, Mike peered directly into a pair of dark eyes not much different from the ones belonging to the guy who had seemed on the verge ripping his head off. These ones, however, belonged to one of the prettiest, angriest girls he'd ever seen. She had shoulder-length brown hair, full lips, honey-brown skin, and almond-shaped eyes that appeared to spit fire. Mike opened his mouth to say something, but all he could do was move his lips up and down like a fish trying to breathe in shallow water.

The girl shook her head. "You southern kids are so pathetic. You picked the wrong guy to tick off on your first day in Inuvik. Good luck, because he's going to be in some of your classes, and sooner or later he's going to make your life miserable." She didn't speak the words; she hurled them. Then, with a flip of her hair and without making any attempt to avoid Mike's books, she stomped on the scattered papers and stalked off.

Mike slumped to the floor. Leaning against the closest locker, he tipped the back of his head against the cold metal, closed his eyes, and sighed profoundly. What a nightmare! He didn't know how long he stayed in that position, but part of him wanted to believe that if he shut his eyes long enough, he'd be back in St. Albert when he opened them.

"You're not going to cry, are you?"

Mike heard the voice but didn't open his eyes. He didn't want the next chapter of his nightmare to begin.

"The last guy Gwen Thrasher talked to cried. Of course, she broke his nose right before she talked to him, but he cried. He bawled, actually. No, it was more like sobbing and snuffling. Really pathetic. He was from the South, too. For some reason she really hates guys from the South. You're from the South, aren't you? You look kind of brown to be from the South, but you seem like you're from the South. You're too …

I don't know … helpless to be from up north. You're not Dene or Inuvialuit, anyway. What are you? East Indian? Mexican? Some kind of Caribbean, Rastafarian rap guy? Oh, I know! You're some type of Mongolian, Sherpa, South American dude! Maybe Bolivian or Colombian. Your dad's some big drug warlord who had to move to the other end of the world to escape a big drug cartel war and threats on your life."

Mike couldn't take it anymore. The voice just wouldn't stop. This was a different type of nightmare altogether. He opened his eyes to see who was verbally attacking him. A pair of large brown eyes stared down at him from thick black-rimmed glasses perched on two chubby brown cheeks. The boy likely stood the same height as Mike, but he was twice as big around. He had a bristly shock of closely cropped black hair that accentuated the roundness of his face. When he spoke, his eyes got larger with each word.

"You could be from Fiji. There are dark dudes in Fiji. No, that's not it. You're the descendant of some Aboriginal king from the outback of Australia. 'Good day, mate! Want to see my 'roo?' I think Australia's pretty much the coolest place in the world. Well, cool not in a temperature way, because Inuvik is one of the coolest places that way. I mean, cool in every other way. Aren't marsupials the coolest animals on the planet? Pouches! How many animals have pouches? They say a baby kangaroo is no bigger than a worm when it's born and it has to crawl to its mother's pouch without falling off with all that hopping and crap. Jeez, that's unreal!"

"Okay!" Mike cried. "Stop! I mean, please stop!" He immediately felt bad when the big boy's face clouded. "Look, I'm sorry. I didn't mean to yell. It's just that I've had a terrible morning, and, well, I can't really even catch my breath to say anything because you're talking so much and so fast."

The big boy's eyes widened behind his glasses, and a huge grin returned to his face. "I'm Donnie Debastien." He extended his hand.

Mike smiled back. Hesitating, he sighed and gripped the boy's hand, pulling and hoisting himself to his feet. "This just hasn't been my day," he said, sighing.

"And the morning isn't even over."

Mike grimaced. "Thanks, Donnie. That makes me feel a whole lot better. By the way, my name's Mike Watson."

Donnie blinked. "Well, look at it this way, Mike. You've already done battle with Monster Kiktorak *and* Gwen Thrasher. It doesn't get any worse or scarier than that. From here on it's pretty easy."

"Monster Kiktorak?"

Donnie nodded solemnly. "Joseph Kiktorak. He's one mean dude. Hates everybody just as much as you, so you don't need to feel special or anything."

Mike started gathering the papers still scattered on the floor. "You know what, Donnie? As strange as this might seem, that actually *does* make me feel better. I guess that just shows how bad my day's gone so far. What's that guy's problem, anyway?"

Donnie tried to bend at the waist and help, but his ample belly wouldn't let him double over. With a sigh he lowered himself to his knees and began assisting Mike. "Well, I guess Joseph's had it pretty rough. His mom and dad split up a couple of years ago. His dad moved back to Tuktoyaktuk. That's where he's from. Then his mom took a job in Cambridge Bay in Nunavut. That meant Joseph had to start living with his granny. She's really nice and all, but it just isn't the same as having a mom or dad around. He seems to be angry at everyone and everything now. It's kind of hard on his granny because he seems to get in some new trouble every second week." Donnie paused for a moment, then shook his head. "You think he'd learn. I mean, he's almost two metres tall, for Pete's sake. How do you do bad crap and expect not to be noticed when you're our age and that tall? Duh!"

Mike nodded and fought the urge to laugh. Not

because he found what had happened to Joseph funny. That was all pretty serious, and considering the guy wanted to kill him, it was dead serious. It was just that Donnie's eyes got so big and he moved his arms around in such an animated fashion that he resembled a funny cartoon character. A lovable and *big* cartoon character. Mike figured that Donnie was likely considered a bit of a nerd by everyone else in Inuvik, but he liked the guy already.

"That's pretty crappy about Joseph," Mike said. "If my parents broke up, I don't know what I'd do. It's hard to even think about."

Donnie was about to say something when the bell rang harshly, making both boys jump.

Grabbing the rest of his books, Mike said, "Hey, Donnie, it was great to meet you."

Donnie nodded, his eyes reaching a new record for big and wide. "Maybe we could do something after school?"

Mike was already hurrying down the hall. "Yeah, that sounds good," he said over his shoulder. "I'll find you later." Reaching the end of the hall, he quickly darted around the corner.

CHAPTER 7

The rest of the school day was pretty ordinary. No more Joseph Kiktorak or Gwen Thrasher. No more embarrassing moments. Mike managed to sit through classes quietly after brief introductions, then slipped out before anyone had a chance to confront him. He also succeeded in keeping his head up and didn't run into any new problems along the way.

When the final buzzer rang, Mike considered searching for Donnie but quickly changed his mind. He was standing by the front doors, trying to decide what to do when someone slammed into his shoulder. His first reaction was to say he was sorry to whoever it was, even though the collision hadn't been his fault. Then he saw Gwen angrily glancing over her shoulder as she bulled through the doors. How could someone so pretty be so bitter about everything? Mike wondered.

He took that as a sign and decided not to push his luck by waiting to see if Donnie wandered by. Mike had survived his first day ... barely. As he walked home, the big moon boots on his feet crunched loudly on the snow, and his breath floated in front of him before trailing around the sides of his head.

One day. Two enemies. One kind of friend. Nice teacher. No homework. Pretty sizable accomplishments for a first day. A lifetime in St. Albert hadn't resulted in a single enemy, so two in one day had to be some kind of world record. And Donnie, well, he seemed pretty nice, but Mike remembered someone saying that the first person you met in a new place was usually a misfit or a nerd supreme. He was fairly certain Donnie met both of those descriptions. But he still liked the guy. Every time those huge eyes almost burst out of their sockets behind those thick glasses, Mike couldn't help but smile with real fondness for the kid.

When Mike reached his new home, he spied his father getting into an RCMP pickup. Then he caught sight of the two snowmobiles sitting on the driveway.

"Hey!" Mike greeted his father.

"Hey, yourself." When Ben noticed Mike grinning at the snowmobiles, he added, "Maybe we can take them out for a spin in a couple of weeks."

"A couple of weeks! That long?"

"Look, Mike, they have to be insured and licensed before we can run them in town. That takes time, and being new here means I have heaps of work to do. Speaking of which, I have to get going." He started to pull out of the driveway. "I'll see you at supper."

Mike sat down heavily on the snowmobile closest to him. It was a Yamaha, while the other one was a bright blue Polaris. The Yamaha had a long body and looked like a working machine. The sleeker Polaris had white racing stripes on its sides.

"The Polaris will be fast for sure."

Mike glanced up and spotted Victor Allen standing in the nearby police yard. "Hi, Mr. Allen. It does look pretty fast."

"They're both nice machines. The Yamaha has a long track and will be excellent for pulling a sled. The Polaris, though, will be fast and fun to drive."

Mike tried to smile, but he was still unhappy about having to wait so long to try out the snowmobiles.

"You know, I have a Polaris pretty much the same as that one. Maybe if I asked your father, I could take you out for a spin sometime soon."

Mike sat up straight. "Really?"

Victor laughed. "Really. I'll talk to your dad tomorrow. Now your mom needs help with some unpacking, so you better head in to see what you can do." He turned and walked toward the police station.

Mike entered the house through the back door. Kicking off his boots, he shrugged out of his parka and let it fall to the floor.

"Mike, is that you?" his mother called from somewhere deep inside the house.

"Yeah, Mom!"

"Put your boots on the mat and pick up your parka. Then come upstairs. I need help deciding where to hang the last of these pictures."

"Jeez!" He stooped to pick up the heavy coat. Between Victor and his mother, he was beginning to think he was surrounded by psychics.

Supper that night was quiet. Ben had to work late, so it was just Mike and his mother. Jeannie tried her best to lighten the mood and get Mike to talk. She described her first trip to the Northern Store and how expensive everything seemed to be. Maybe, she told her son, the first thing Mike and Ben would have to do once they had the snowmobiles going was shoot a caribou or moose so they could afford to eat. Mike responded with nothing more than grunts and a faint smile.

After supper Mike headed to his room. The guy from the local cable company hadn't come to hook up their television and Internet service yet. He didn't know if cellphones and texting worked in Inuvik. Even if they did, he didn't know anyone here to call or text, and that sucked! No friends, no TV, no Internet, no text messaging. They *were* at the end of the Earth!

Mike threw himself onto his bed and stared at the ceiling. The walls were so short due to the steepness of the roof that he was actually looking at the posters and pictures he'd tacked up yesterday. There was a classic image of goaltender Patrick Roy in a Montreal Canadiens uniform, a poster Mike's dad had given him. LeBron James in full flight, mouth open, seemed about to fly over a basketball hoop. Gary Gait, one of the greatest lacrosse players of all time, followed through on a shot while playing with the Colorado Mammoth of the National Lacrosse League. The last picture was perfect. It was so clear that it was almost surreal. It had been taken over Gait's shoulder after he took the shot. You could follow the path the ball took after it left Gait's stick, then see it as it bulged the mesh of the net just over the goalie's shoulder.

Next, his eyes settled on all the athletic accolades he'd accumulated through the years — participation medals, trophies from tournaments, gold medals, most valuable player awards. There was a picture of Mike that had been taken at the Jack Crosby Tournament in Burnaby, British Columbia, when he was a novice. It showed him following through on a shot he'd just taken at the net. They had won that tournament. It was the first time a team from St. Albert had won a major competition outside Alberta, and the banner with Mike's name and the rest of the gang still hung from the rafters of the Kinnex Arena in St. Albert. Mike had played lacrosse with the same bunch of guys for years, and now all of that was over.

He rolled onto his side and took a deep breath. His eyes settled on an object sitting on the bedside table. It was getting dark in the room, so he reached over and clicked on the small bedside lamp.

The object he'd noticed was a shortwave radio. His father had given it to him before they left St. Albert. His mother must have unpacked it today and put it in his room. Mike had been so upset with his father and about the move that he hadn't even thanked him for it. He had simply stuck it in the bottom of a box and piled books and other items on top.

Mike's father had told him he'd had a similar

shortwave radio when he was a kid on the farm and that on cold winter nights he could pick up radio stations and signals from around the world. Ben had said it would be fun to play around with the shortwave in Inuvik. A radio! Fun to play with! To Mike it represented everything that had gone wrong with this life. No friends, no lacrosse, no TV, no computer, no texting. Nothing but a radio and cold winter nights. Nothing at all. *Nothing.*

With a surge of pent-up rage, Mike smashed a clenched fist into the radio. The shortwave spun into the air, stopped abruptly as it reached the end of its cord, clattered off the wall, and fell to the floor with a resounding thud. One of its knobs broke free from the impact, popped off the chair, and disappeared under the dresser.

"Hey!" he heard his dad holler from downstairs. Mike hadn't heard him come home.

"You okay up there, Mike?" Ben asked from the bottom of the stairs.

"Yeah."

"How was school today?"

"Okay."

"Just okay?"

"It was okay."

"Make any friends? Find a girlfriend?"

"Dad!"

"Okay, Mike, I won't bug you. First day is always hard. I'll pop in to say good-night when I come up."

Mike didn't respond, and after a moment or two, he heard his father move away from the bottom of the stairs and head back into the kitchen. There was silence for a moment and then the murmur of voices as his parents began to talk.

Mike lay quietly on the bed and thought about his day. Donnie was sort of a friend. A weird one, but at least he didn't hate Mike. And Gwen was a girl, but she sure wasn't a friend. Man, she had an attitude. Then there was Monster Kiktorak. How could someone fourteen years old be so big and have such a chip on his shoulder? The guy could kill Mike if he really wanted to. Mike shifted his eyes around the room, and once more they fixed on the shortwave radio that now lay on the floor.

Slowly, he sat up, then got to his feet and picked up the radio. After he put it back on the nightstand, he squatted in front of the dresser and groped underneath it for the missing knob. He stretched a little farther, closed his hand around the knob, and pulled it out. Returning to the bed, he sat and flipped the radio back and forth until he spotted the stub where the knob had once been. Luckily, it wasn't broken. The knob had simply popped off the stub that controlled the volume. Fumbling, Mike moved the knob across the stub until the opening caught and it sank back into place. He returned the radio to the nightstand and moved his hand along the cord. Grabbing the plug, he bent over and pushed it into the outlet between the bed and the nightstand. Then, sitting back, he stared at the radio as if it were a fearsome creature that might suddenly leap for his throat.

A radio! How desperate had his life become? Who listened to radio these days? Shrugging, he leaned forward and flicked on the power button. Static. What did he expect? They were at the top of the world. Picking up the radio, he placed it in his lap and studied the buttons: power, volume, tuning, some kind of "band" thing, and a spot for an antenna wire. The thing likely wouldn't work without some kind of antenna. Just his luck. Not wanting to give up just yet, Mike took the tuning knob between his thumb and forefinger and twirled it.

He had barely moved the knob when voices shot through the static. They spoke a different language, but it was amazingly clear. He listened closer. It sounded like Chinese. After a few seconds, he adjusted the knob again and another voice crackled through. This time there was no mistaking the language. It was Russian, a tongue he'd heard before. Holy crap! The voice took on a sinister tone. Some kind of spy broadcast! Sending secret messages across the top of the world?

Mike rotated the knob again, then stopped abruptly. There was no mistaking the tone of an excited sportscaster in the middle of a play-by-play. He bent down and pulled the radio close to his ear. It was a basketball game coming all the way from Madison Square Garden. The Knicks and the Philadelphia 76ers. Mike loved all sports, and in his own right wasn't that bad a basketball player. He listened hard as the play-by-play man called the game, picturing the crowd at the fabled arena as the Knicks sank a basket and hustled back on defence.

If he picked up a Knicks game that easily, what else could he find? He spun the knob. The number of stations was amazing. With every little turn he hit another one. He was obviously picking them up from all over the world because the languages sounded very different. Russian, Chinese, German, French, Spanish — it didn't stop!

Then a station made him halt in his tracks. A hockey game! And it was coming from Rexall Place in Edmonton. The Oilers were hosting the Anaheim Ducks, and Edmonton was up two goals. Carefully putting the radio down, Mike settled back against his pillow and listened. He had been to Oiler games and to Edmonton Rush lacrosse matches at Rexall Place and could easily visualize the usual sold-out crowd. He closed his eyes and listened as the announcer's voice rose and fell with the tempo of the play. The Oilers scored again, and he pumped his fist in the dark, whispering a barely audible *"Yes!"* Then he tensed as Anaheim began to control the puck and dominate on a power play. An *"Awwww!"* escaped his lips along with the crowd on the radio as the Ducks scored with three minutes left in the game.

The teams lined up for the next faceoff, and Mike pictured the championship banners that hung from Rexall Place's rafters, along with the retired jerseys of guys like Wayne Gretzky who had played for Stanley Cup teams of the past. He suffered with the crowd as the final seconds ticked down. The Ducks pulled their goalie, and there was a mad scramble as the buzzer sounded to end the game.

Mike waited patently to hear the three stars. He faintly heard the name of the third star, but it was somewhere off in the distance. His mind floated up to the banners high in the rink's rafters. He saw Donnie's huge eyes bulging at him and then the beautiful but harsh features of Gwen Thrasher. Her face faded and morphed into the hateful countenance of

Joseph Kiktorak. The Monster moved closer, and in slow motion grabbed Mike by the front of his shirt. The hulking kid laughed and brought his smirking face closer and closer to Mike's until sleep smothered all conscious thought.

CHAPTER 8

The next few days went well at school. Joseph Kiktorak and Gwen Thrasher weren't in any of Mike's classes, so he could actually relax somewhat. Thankfully, he didn't run into Joseph in the halls, either. Donnie told him that the big kid had been missing from school for a couple of days and nobody really knew what was going on. Mike did see Gwen a few times and tried to look in the other direction or duck behind the crowd in the hall. When their eyes did meet on one occasion, Mike swore he saw sparks shoot from those smouldering orbs. The intensity was too much to bear, and he had to glance away immediately. Despite her hostility, the frustrating part was that Mike knew he had a bit of a crush on her. What was he thinking?

Donnie, on the other hand, was turning into a good friend. Mike realized Donnie was something of an outcast, but he didn't care. He had always been popular in St. Albert, yet that hadn't stopped him from hanging out with guys who didn't fit the star athlete mould. As long as someone was fun to be with, it didn't matter to Mike if they were a science nerd, book geek, artsy weirdo, or goth. If they had a sense of humour and didn't hurt anybody, he didn't care. The guys on the lacrosse team had understood that about Mike and it never weakened their friendship.

Mike's mom and dad had told him that one of the best ways to break through barriers and make friends was through sports. With that in mind he had signed up for intramural basketball. He knew from gym class that he matched up pretty well with the other guys skill-wise, so he didn't figure he had any embarrassment in store for him. Donnie thought it was a pretty good idea, too. He told Mike that sometimes people were a little slow to accept newcomers from the South, but once they showed they were regular guys, everything was usually okay. It was the "usually" part that worried Mike.

On Friday, Mike checked the bulletin board outside the gym and saw he'd been placed on what looked like a pretty good team. Apparently, they played three games at a time across the gym instead of lengthwise

— four players aside, eight players per team. Two twenty-minute games were played during lunchtime. He knew Mitchell Firth, Tommy Aleekuk, and Tyler Snowshoe from gym class, and they were all quite good. Tommy was Inuvialuit and a superb athlete. Despite his short, stocky stature, he was an amazing jumper. Mike had been astounded when Tommy, who wasn't even a metre and half tall, had touched the rim with his fingers just fooling around in gym class.

After changing into shorts and a T-shirt, Mike wandered into the gym and spotted his group getting ready on the first court. He recognized some of the guys on the other team and remembered from the standings that were posted outside the gym that they were in second place overall, while Mike's team was in fifth. They must be good. After awkward nods and "Heys!" from his guys, Mike sat down and watched the first shift.

It was really fast-paced, and it was clear that Tommy and Bobby Vittrekwa from the other team were the two best players on the floor. Tommy was incredibly quick. Short and muscular, his compact strength, much like Mike's, made him hard to stop. And what a jumper! He would leave the floor in mid-stride and soar waist-high on his opponents before releasing the ball to the net. Once he was airborne, he seemed to hang in slow motion the way Michael Jordan and LeBron James did in the DVDs Mike had seen.

Bobby was smooth as glass. Long-limbed and fluid in his stride, he was Gwich'in Dene and originally from Fort McPherson. Once he was running, he seemed to mesmerize anyone he matched up against. His long strides made him deceptive, and though he didn't seem fast, he'd flow past the guys on Mike's team as if they were standing still. He also had the uncanny knack of knowing exactly where he was in relation to the net. Without looking over his shoulder he'd blindly spin in the air and seemingly release the ball before he focused on the hoop, making it fall through the net with a *swoosh*.

Mike did well, posting up and dropping the ball through several times on each of his first few shifts. He could sense the guys warming up to him as they became more aware of his ability and skill on the court. On more than one occasion Tommy slapped Mike's hand as he ran back after sinking a basket, smiling and nodding as they passed. Bobby, too, was a good sport and grinned and shook his head a couple of times when Mike kept him away from the net.

The game came down to the last possession, and when Mike made a blind pass behind his back to Tommy, who left his feet and finger-rolled the ball in, the guys jumped off the bench and whooped with excitement.

"You da man!" Donnie yelled from the stands. Mike's new friend leaped to his feet, arms in the air, eyes on the verge of exploding behind his glasses.

It was the game winner, and everybody high-fived before they shook hands with the other team.

Bobby didn't take Mike's hand as they came together. Instead, he nodded and patted Mike on the shoulder. "You got game, buddy. The rest of the year's going to be a whole lot different with you and Tommy playing together. It was bad enough playing against one tank. Now I have to face two at a time."

"You better believe it," Tommy said as he looped his arm around Mike's neck. "But now the fun begins." He stared at something over Mike's shoulder. "They're in first place, and she's *aaaaall* yours!"

Mike had a sinking feeling as he slowly turned to face the other direction. "Oh ... my ... God."

The other team was warming up, and right in the middle of the group stood Gwen Thrasher, who looked even more intimidating in her gym gear. She wore a black T-shirt with the sleeves cut back, revealing her arms from shoulders to fingertips. The sinews in her arms stood out with every move and twist. Her triceps were exceptionally defined and rippled every time she caught or shot the ball. She wore baggy red knee-length shorts that on many guys would have made their calves appear small. Not in her case. As she ran and jumped, the muscles at the backs of her legs balled up and seemed to explode.

After running in for a layup, she curled under the net, spied Mike, slowed down, and stopped. Her dark, seething eyes locked on his, and for a second Mike thought he was going to collapse on the cold gym floor. He wasn't sure if it was from fear or from the overwhelming feeling that his heart was going to detonate in his chest. Her stare seemed to last forever, then with a flip of her shoulder-length hair she turned and sprinted to the back of the line.

"Jeez, I'm glad I'm not you," Tommy whispered.

"Man, I wish I didn't have to play another game," Bobby said. "How will I concentrate knowing Gwen will be chewing you up one court over." With that he clapped Mike on the back and jogged to join his team at the other end of the gym.

Mike took a deep breath and ambled over to the court with Tommy, Mitchell, Tyler, and the other guys.

Gwen's team looked good. They had at least three guys Mike thought were better than most of the boys on their team, including him. And then there was Gwen. She sank everything she tossed during the warm-up and carried herself in a confident and athletic manner. This was going to be a difficult game.

When the whistle blew, Gwen stayed on the floor.

"Okay, Mike, I'm going to save your butt," Tommy said with a smirk. "Wait for the second shift. Let's see how this goes."

Tommy strode confidently onto the floor. He won the jump ball to start the game, but they didn't win much after that. Gwen wasn't as strong as the boys were, and she wasn't the best player on the floor, but what she lacked in those departments she more than made up with her hustle and determination. There wasn't a loose ball or a hard battle that she lost. If it meant diving, she dived. If it meant standing her ground and getting hit, she stood firm. And if it meant clearing a crowd while she had possession of the ball, her elbows were up and she cleared the house. Gwen was the grittiest player Mike had ever seen.

Tommy came to the bench, gulping for air; the team was already down eight points. "Man, is she on it today. Something tells me it's got something to do with you being on our team. She's going to kill me if she keeps this up."

Mike nodded but didn't speak as he headed onto the floor. The other team was tough and played a very physical style under the net. Playing with Mitchell and

Tyler this game, Mike and his teammates worked the ball around the perimeter. Mitchell and Tyler had terrific mid-distance shots, and Mike was a great playmaker. They moved the ball around the outside until they had clear shots, then hustled back and shut the other team down on defence. By the time their shift ended, the game was tied. Tommy nodded his approval and slapped Mike's hand as he headed back onto the floor.

The game continued to be a hard-fought contest. Tommy made some incredible acrobatic manoeuvres, but Gwen and the other team gave him fits with their physical style and rough play. Mike, Mitchell, and Tyler hit the floor and methodically drove the ball up the court, then Mike broke through the perimeter and passed the ball off to one of the other guys who had a clear shot. They kept chewing into the other team's lead, keeping within two points each time out.

It was late in the game when Tommy came gasping to the bench. "I can't keep this up. They're keying on me every time, and that Nasogaloak kid keeps sticking his elbows in my ribs under the net. I'm so sore I can hardly breathe."

"This is likely the last shift, Tommy," Mike said. "We'll take care of it. C'mon, Ty! Let's go, Mitchell!"

Mike jogged out to the floor and stopped. Gwen was bent over with her hands on her knees at centre court. She was skipping a rest with her line to face him for the last shift of the game. He slowed as he approached her and stopped. "Hey, Gwen."

Surprise registered on her face. Then, regaining her composure, she squinted and crouched into position for the jump ball, the muscles in her arms standing out on her dark skin under a sheen of sweat.

Nervously, Mike glanced at the crowd, which had grown as the games had progressed. The gym was packed now, and everyone's attention was riveted on Mike's game. He spotted Donnie at the top of the bleachers. The big kid's eyes were so big they seemed to spill out past the sides of his glasses onto the folds of his chubby cheeks. Donnie was nervously chewing his nails and waved weakly when Mike glanced in his direction. Turning back to Gwen, Mike crouched low and focused on the ball in the outstretched hand of the referee.

The ball was up! Mike sprang and swatted it over to Tyler. Gwen gave him an unnecessary shove on the chest, then rushed back into her own zone to defend against their attack. The shift was fast, furious, and brutally physical. Every time Mike had the ball, Gwen was in his face. He could see her watching his eyes or keying on his chest to anticipate his moves, which she did without fail. Even if he got a slight jump on her, she deftly hooked an arm or managed to subtly stick an elbow into his midsection.

In Mike's mind the other players disappeared. It was just Gwen and him. When she had the ball, he was with her every step. And every time he moved too close she roughly held him off. When she had the ball, she gave him short rib shots with her elbows at every opportunity. When the referee yelled that there was one minute left, Mike's side was down by two points.

Mike, Mitchell, and Tyler slowly moved the ball down the court, systematically moving it back and forth. They had steadily gained a rhythm throughout the game and now played comfortably with one another. Although Gwen was watching him closely, Mike sensed the other team respected his playmaking skills and expected him to dish the ball once he gained position near their net. They wouldn't anticipate a shot.

The boys continued to pass, moving the ball closer and closer to the net. Mike feigned moving the ball to Mitchell, then drove inside to the net. Gwen was with him all the way. He stopped suddenly and pretended to pass across to Tyler. Everyone went for the fake except Gwen. As Mike left his feet for the shot, he felt a sharp impact and pain as Gwen rammed her elbow deep into his ribs. When the ball left his hands, his right arm involuntarily dropped with the pain. The ball arced toward the net, bounced off the right side of the rim, and harmlessly skidded out of bounds as the whistle blew.

Mike doubled over, holding his ribs. It had been a blatant foul. Gwen and her team were exchanging high fives at the side of the net as Mike's team wandered listlessly over to their bench. Mike struggled upright and made his way to join his fellow players.

"Jeez, that was rough," Tommy said. "You made the right move, man. There's no way the ref should've let that go, but he missed it. G.T.'s got an attitude, that's for sure. But I think she likes you." He laughed when he saw the amazed expression on Mike's face. "Hey, if she really hated you, that elbow would've been aimed a little lower or a little higher. I think it's love!" He grabbed Mike around the neck.

Despite his embarrassment, Mike enjoyed the camaraderie and chuckled sheepishly.

The two teams lined up facing each other in single file and moved forward to shake hands. When Mike passed Gwen, she glanced away and slapped his hand a little too hard to be friendly. Mike caught Tommy's eye, and his teammate blew him a kiss. Mock-scowling, Mike shook his head.

"Man, that was something else!" Donnie burbled as he rushed up to Mike on the way to the change room. "I think Gwen likes you," he added, taking off his glasses to wipe them on his T-shirt.

"Jeez, Donnie, that's what Tommy just said. You guys are nuts. Didn't you see what she did to me? She absolutely hates me. Whenever she looks at me, I expect her to spit or throw up or worse."

Donnie replaced his glasses, his eyes once more wide with excitement. "Man, you don't understand girls at all, do you? And we're talking about G.T., you know."

"And, Donnie, I suppose in your vast experience with girls, you picked up the fact that a shot to the ribs means a girl likes you?"

"Well, no. Obviously, I'm not an expert." Donnie hesitated, looking slightly hurt. "But I do know G.T. I've known her since we were kids. If you were any other guy from the South, and if she really hated you, she'd have elbowed you somewhere pretty tender. That elbow to the ribs was her way of saying, 'I think you're a good athlete and I sort of like you.'"

Realizing he'd hurt the big guy's feelings, Mike gave Donnie a friendly jab. "Well, Donnie, I think you don't know what the heck you're talking about, but I'm glad you're on my side and came out to watch the game. It made me feel pretty good to see a friend up in the stands."

When Donnie glanced up, there was no mistaking the happiness in his eyes. "Do you mean that, Mike? I'm your friend. I mean, you're a jock and stuff and I'm, well, kind of ... kind of ..."

"Kind of fun to hang around with," Mike finished for him. "Look, do you know Victor Allen?"

"Jeez, Mike, who doesn't? He's one of the most respected elders in Inuvik."

"Well, Donnie, he said he might take me out snow-mobiling this weekend. If it's okay with him, and if you're not busy doing something else, would you like to come with us?"

Now Donnie didn't even attempt to hide his feelings. "Would I ever!"

Mike patted Donnie on the back, then ran to the locker room to change.

CHAPTER 9

True to his word, Victor spoke to Ben, who agreed to let him take Mike out for a snowmobile ride on Sunday. Saturday seemed to last an eternity. Ben and Jeannie tried to keep Mike busy helping with the last of the unpacking, but that didn't work. After finding the tenth item that Mike had misplaced despite clear instructions, Jeannie gave up. He was simply too excited and preoccupied to be of any use.

So after what seemed to be the longest day and night of his life, Mike stood beside Donnie at the side door on Sunday morning, peering out, anxiously waiting for Victor to arrive. It was a beautiful sunny day, and the outside thermometer said it was only minus thirteen.

Mike moaned. "Jeez, what's taking them so long?"

"It's only 9:30, Mike. Didn't Victor tell your dad we'd leave at about 10:00?"

"Yeah, but you never know. He could get here early."

"Mike, this is the North. We relax up here when we do stuff. We don't worry if we leave exactly on time. We leave when we leave. A trip out of town or to camp is supposed to be relaxing and take your mind off things. If we leave by 10:30 or 11:00, no one's going to be too upset."

Mike gasped. "Don't say that. I'll go nuts if it takes that long."

"You got TV yesterday, didn't you? Let's watch something. It's got to be better than staring out the window."

Mike knew Donnie was right. He walked over and turned on the television. They had cable now, so he flipped around the channels until he found some old Spider-Man cartoons.

"Man, I love these!" Donnie cried, flopping onto the couch. "These old-school cartoons are so cool. I mean, I like the Spider-Man movies, too, but these are great. They're kind of cool but funny at the same time. Do you read comics?"

Mike had settled onto the couch beside Donnie and opened his mouth to reply.

"Man, I read comics all the time," Donnie continued. "You can't really get them up here, but my uncle in Edmonton sends me bunches every month. Spider-Man, Iron Man, Fantastic Four, The Hulk, Moon Knight, New Universal, Daredevil, you name it. They even have comics based on Stephen King novels now. Did you know that?"

Mike thought about replying, but Donnie kept going.

"The Stephen King ones are kind of creepy, but the graphics are incredible. Daredevil's pretty amazing, too. I don't know why the movie didn't do better. I bet if a better actor had played the lead role ..."

Mike smiled. Once Donnie got started, there was no stopping him. He half listened and half watched Spider-Man swing across the screen in old-style black and white, trying to catch up to Dr. Octopus as the villain sprang from building to building using mechanical arms. Donnie began to fade in and out as Mike daydreamed.

"I like the way some of the old characters look better in the cartoons than in the movies. Doc Oc, for sure. Man, he looks so cool in black and white. In the movie he ... and I mean you never see Spider-Man kiss anybody in the cartoon. Why does he have to kiss his girlfriend in the movie? He kisses his aunt on the cheek, but a girl on the lips? That just doesn't cut it, man! What if he didn't kiss her in ... Rhino was the baddest guy of all. Why don't they show him in the movie? Look at him! Right there in black and white!"

Mike focused on the TV in time to see Rhino head-butt his way through a brick wall.

"He looks so bad in black and white," Donnie went on. "Imagine him in a movie. Hey, I could play Rhino. I'm kind of built for the part, don't you think? I could bust through walls and be pretty famous at the same time. Spidey would have his work cut out for him, man! I could take on ..."

Mike didn't know how long they sat like that — Donnie talking and him half paying attention — but the sound of a horn in the driveway snapped him back to life. He jumped to the window and saw Victor stepping out of a pickup truck. Two snowmobiles, one pulling a sled, drove in beside the truck.

"Let's go, Donnie."

Getting up, Donnie glanced at his watch and smiled. "Ten-fifteen. Man, am I good, or am I good? I knew there was no way we'd be leaving at 10:00. We'll be lucky to get out of here by 10:30."

"Oh, shut up, show-off, and let's get out of here." Mike rushed past Donnie to get into his coat and boots at the back door. "Mom, we're going now!"

"Okay, Mike!" she shouted back. "Be careful. Say hi and thank Mr. Allen for me."

"Okay," Mike said as he raced out the back door. When he approached Victor, he slowed to a walk. "*Qanaqitpit*, Mr. Allen."

Hearing Mike's greeting, Victor grinned ear to ear. "*Nakuurunga*, Mike. And I'm Victor, not Mr. Allen." He put an arm around Mike's shoulders.

"Okay … Victor."

Victor looked over Mike's shoulder. "And how are you, Donnie?"

Donnie was slowly approaching, a bit out of breath from hurriedly getting ready and trying to keep up with Mike. "Oh, I'm pretty good, Victor."

"Mike, I want you to meet three of my grand-daughters — Melissa, Trish, and Claudine. Girls, this is Mike. And, of course, you know Donnie Debastien."

Mike gazed shyly at the three girls bundled up in snow pants, parkas, and the cool boots he still needed to find out about. "Hey, Melissa, Claudine, Trish."

"Hey, Mike!" the three girls chorused.

"Hey, *Dawwwwwnie*," Melissa drawled, smirking at Donnie.

"Hi, Claudine, Trish," Donnie said, avoiding eye contact with Melissa. Leaning in close to Mike, he whispered, "Melissa picks on me. Well, she picks on me more than most people, since most people pick on me at least a little. She's the worst, though. She tried to pull my pants down in gym class once. She ended up pulling down my underwear at the same time."

Mike suppressed a laugh, then turned back to Victor. "I keep forgetting to ask you, Victor. What are those boots called that I see people wearing?" He pointed at Victor's and the girls' feet.

"Those are kamiks, Mike. The Gwich'in call them mukluks."

"I could've told you that," Donnie whispered in Mike's ear.

"They're light as a feather and warmer than warm," Victor continued. "They can be made of different skin or material and have a duffle type liner inside. It almost feels like walking in your socks. People who live by the ocean have the bottom part made of seal so they're waterproof." Victor glanced at Mike's feet and smiled. "But lots of people wear those moon boots now. Kind of nice to have both. But I still prefer kamiks."

Mike made a mental note that he had to find a way to get a pair so he could toss the moon boots.

"Okay," Victor said, "we have a two-hour ride both ways, so we better get going. It's nice and warm today, but we don't want to get back too late after dark. We're going to Reindeer Station." He motioned to one of the snowmobiles in the driveway. "The reason I drove over here in the pickup, Mike, is because I talked to your dad. He says if I take your Polaris out of town, you can drive part of the way."

It was Mike's turn to smile ear to ear.

Victor held a small ignition key in the air. "I'll ride with Mike. Trish and Claudine will ride together. Donnie, you ride with Mulluk." Seeing puzzlement on Mike's face, Victor added, "Mulluk is Melissa's Inuvialuit name."

All three girls snickered when they noticed Donnie's look of horror.

Victor pulled the cover off the Polaris and tossed it aside. The back of the snowmobile was raised on a piece of wood. He lifted the back, removed the wood, and dropped the snowmobile onto the snow. "If you don't keep the track off the snow, it can freeze and get ruined or at least make it hard to get going," he explained to Mike.

Mike watched Victor intently as he popped a button out from the snowmobile's dashboard and tugged the pull-start rope. *Brrrrrrrrrr!* The engine turned over reluctantly.

"It's pretty warm today, so it should start easy," Victor said. "You still need to pull out the choke." He pointed at the button he'd left slightly out on the dash.

Grabbing the rope in both hands, he yanked it rapidly several times. *Brrrrrrrrr, brrrrrrrrrr, brrrrrrrrrr, brrrrrrrr-vrooooooom-puttt-puttttttt-puttttt!* Victor released the rope and squeezed the throttle repeatedly. The engine ignited and began to idle until he pushed the choke back into the dash.

Nodding at Mike, Victor hopped onto the snowmobile and placed one knee on the seat and the other foot on the running board so that he half stood, half knelt on the machine. He squeezed the throttle again and drove the machine in a large circle out onto the lawn, then doubled back and halted beside Mike.

The smell of gas fumes and smoky hide filled Mike's nostrils. Seeing Trish climb on behind Claudine, Mike slid onto the Polaris behind Victor. All eyes were on Donnie as he stared back at the house, seemingly frozen.

"Dawwwwwnie!"

Donnie pursed his lips at the sound of Mulluk's voice. As he turned to face the group, Mulluk patted the seat behind her. "Come on, Donnie, don't be shy. You can wrap your arms around me if you want and hold on tight."

Donnie swallowed hard.

"Donnie, climb on with Mulluk," Victor said. "The skidoo has a backrest and two handgrips beside the seat. It's a comfortable ride."

Avoiding eye contact, Donnie moved past Mulluk, climbed onto the seat behind her, and found the handgrips as quickly as possible. Wrapping his fingers around them, he leaned against the backrest and shut his eyes. Claudine giggled uncontrollably as she pulled her machine around onto the lawn the way Victor had, but instead of doubling back she zipped down the street. Mulluk pulled past, and Mike caught a glimpse of Donnie, who gave him one of the most pathetic looks imaginable. Even though he felt sorry for the guy, Mike had to turn away and laugh. Victor revved the engine, and they fell in behind the other two snowmobiles.

Although it was warmer, sunny, and clear, the temperature was still minus thirteen. Mike's face became frigid from the wind created by the snowmobile's speed, and he had to duck for shelter behind Victor every few minutes, holding his head downward and letting his cheeks warm up. When he looked ahead, he saw they were now off the road and winding between houses on a trail that appeared well worn by snowmobile traffic. Sparks flew from under the snowmobiles when they streaked over gravel that had been spread on slippery sections of streets they crossed along the way.

As they passed one last section of buildings, Mike spotted a huge white expanse and knew it was the

Mackenzie River. It stretched out of sight to his left and right — a frozen winter highway. The girls, who had been driving considerably faster than Victor, waited ahead for them on the snow-covered ice. Claudine and Trish smiled and waved as Victor and Mike pulled up. Donnie appeared even more miserable behind Mulluk.

Victor cupped his mouth close to Mike's ear. "I think he's sweet on her."

Mike stifled a laugh as he looked away from Donnie.

Victor shut off his machine, and so did the girls. "Mike, can you see the ice road on the river?"

Mike nodded.

"Trucks, cars, snowmobiles, and tractor-trailers all use the river to get to Aklavik and Tuktoyaktuk. We're going to head downriver on the ice road toward the ocean. Partway, the ice road will cut off, but we'll continue on the main part of the river to Reindeer Station. It's going to take us about two hours, so we better get going. You get cold or have to pee, tap on my shoulder and let me know."

"Okay, Mr. ... Victor," Mike said.

As soon as Victor finished speaking, the girls pull-started their machines and roared off in a cloud of snow. Mulluk hit the throttle with such force that Donnie banged hard against the backrest, his head flopping back, causing the flaps of his fur cap to fly out on both sides. Victor eased their snowmobile into motion, and they were underway.

The trip was unreal. Mike couldn't get over the fact that they were driving on frozen water. A plough had cleared a road on the river, and Mike saw ice whiz by beneath them. In some places the ice was covered in hard-packed snow, but in others he could see the ice. At times it looked black and in other spots it was various shades of blue. There were cracks, too. None were very wide, but they were cracks all the same, zigzagging through the ice and disappearing into the snowbanks on each side of the road. On their right they passed the town, and in contrast to the bright whiteness around them the buildings that at first had appeared drab to him now seemed colourful.

"Tank farm!" Victor shouted over his shoulder, pointing at a group of gigantic, round, cake-like structures on his right. "Barge brings in fuel each fall and it's stored there."

They continued along the river, and soon the town was well out of sight behind them. The Mackenzie was the biggest river Mike had ever seen. It was so wide across that the cabins they passed at odd intervals appeared quite distant and small. Craggy evergreen trees lined the banks, and willows grew thick in some spots. Snowmobile tracks criss-crossed the snow in all directions around the road, and animal tracks dotted the snow toward the bank.

Many of the cabins they passed had wisps of smoke lazily floating up from their chimneys. It reminded Mike of Christmas cards his parents received in the mail each year. He imagined the warmth and coziness inside the cabins as people sat close to the stove, warming their hands and drinking steaming cups of coffee and hot chocolate.

Mike began to enjoy the cold, fresh feeling on his face. He spent longer periods of time gazing past Victor and watching the two snowmobiles leading the way. The girls were having fun and occasionally wove back and forth across the road as if they were navigating an obstacle course. He smiled as he imagined Donnie, wide-eyed, holding on for dear life.

Ahead, he saw where the road veered to the left. Trish and Claudine slowed down and gingerly moved up over the bank instead of making the turn. Mulluk swung wide and began to gather speed, aiming at a point in the snowbank where it appeared other snowmobiles had preceded her. She struck the bank like a skier hitting the ramp of a jump. As the machine left the snow, it seemed suspended for a few seconds in the air. The flaps on Donnie's hat flew high on the sides of his head, and his body lifted gently off the seat. The snowmobile landed hard on the other side, and Donnie hit the seat solidly before bouncing off and tumbling into the snow. Mulluk continued a short distance before pulling to a sudden stop.

Victor shook his head as he sped to the bank and drove the heavy machine up and over. Quickly, Mike and Victor jumped off and hurried to where Donnie lay moaning in the snow. The girls were standing over him, covering their mouths and attempting without success to stifle their giggling. Victor glared at them, and they stopped.

Every part of Donnie, including his face, was covered in powdery snow. He could have been a big doughnut rolled in icing sugar. His glasses had popped onto his forehead, and his short, spiky hair appeared to be layered with ice. The ridiculous cap lay a short distance away, forgotten for the moment.

Victor knelt beside Donnie, took off his own mitten, and placed a hand on the boy's chest. "Take your time, Donnie." He removed the glasses from Donnie's forehead. "You had the wind knocked out of you and need to catch your breath. That's it. Breathe easy. Now try to take deeper breaths." Victor grew quiet as Donnie filled and released his lungs several times. "There. How's that?"

Donnie nodded and slowly opened his eyes. He looked at Victor, then Mike, giving them a weak smile. The snow on his face had melted, and his brown cheeks were wet and bright pink. He glanced at the girls, and his eyes grew wide, almost popping out of his head. "She tried to kill me!" he shouted, pointing at Mulluk.

The girls burst out laughing, but once again grew quiet after a scowl from Victor.

"It was reckless for Mulluk to jump the bank," Victor said, "but she wasn't trying to kill you, Donnie. And she won't do it again, right, Mulluk?"

The girl nodded meekly, and studied her kamiks.

"Now, Donnie, let's get you up." Victor supported Donnie's back and helped him into a sitting position.

Mike retrieved Donnie's hat and handed it to him as he cleaned and replaced his glasses. Donnie stood up, and Victor and Mike helped brush the snow off his parka.

Seeing Donnie pretty much back in one piece, Victor seemed satisfied and nodded. "Okay, let's get going. Donnie, Mulluk will drive carefully the rest of the way."

Claudine and Trish giggled slightly with their heads together as they grabbed each other and sprinted back to their machine.

Donnie stood beside Mike and looked at him with wide-eyed fear. "She won't rest until I'm dead," he whispered, leaning close. "You have to do something. I won't survive the day. Once it gets dark, who knows what she's capable of?"

Mike couldn't help but laugh out loud.

"You need to take this seriously," Donnie said. "You don't know her. Look at her."

Mike watched as Mulluk blew her nose with a piece of tissue paper.

"Thinking, plotting — she's pure evil," Donnie mumbled.

"Look, Donnie, Victor and I will be right behind you. Anything happens, we're right there. We have your back, buddy." Mike put his arm around the big kid. "Now we better get going, or it'll be dark before you know it."

Donnie gripped Mike's arm and nodded with gravity. "Thanks, Mike. If anything *does* happen, tell my mother I love her." With that he turned and glared defiantly at Mulluk as he walked over and sat behind her. Back in the saddle, he gave Mike a tight-lipped, wide-eyed nod and thumbs-up sign.

Mike returned the thumbs-up and trudged back to the idling Polaris.

Victor shook his head. "Young love! Now let's get

going, Mike." He slid to the back of the Polaris's seat, pushing himself tight against the backrest.

Mike's jaw dropped. "You mean …?"

"Take it away, Mike. You saw me. Throttle on the right, brake on the left. Mulluk will behave now, so just follow the girls at a decent speed."

Mike tried not to look too excited, but he knew he was grinning like an idiot. Some of his friends in St. Albert had snowmobiles, but he had always been a passenger, never a driver.

Gingerly climbing in front of Victor, he gripped the handlebars and gave the throttle a little squeeze that only made the engine race. He felt his face heat with embarrassment and gripped the throttle too hard. The machine lurched ahead, almost giving them whiplash.

Victor chuckled and placed a hand on Mike's shoulder. "Easy. Start to squeeze and gradually make it harder. You'll get used to it."

Mike nodded and did what Victor suggested. Sure enough, they moved gradually, then gained speed.

Seeing Mike and Victor go, the girls quickly circled and raced ahead. Mike continued to squeeze the throttle, his heart in his mouth, until they were keeping pace with the other two machines.

"Good driving, Mike!" Victor shouted over his shoulder.

Mike nodded, trying to control his excitement. He smiled as he sped along behind the girls, giddy with the power of the machine as they hurtled across the snow and ice. Was this cool or what?

CHAPTER 10

The rest of the drive to Reindeer Station was one of the best experiences Mike had ever had. As he gained confidence, he swerved into the deeper snow slightly off the trail. A fine powder flew up, sending a cold mist onto his face. Laughing, he closed his eyes and shook his head before veering back onto the trail. They were no longer on the road, of course, but on a trail well worn by snowmobile traffic. The girls sensed that Mike wanted to try new stuff as he gained confidence, so they sped up, slowed down, made sharp turns, and zipped along the edge of snowbanks, keeping their velocity high so the machines tilted slightly on their sides but the force of gravity prevented them from falling over. It was like riding a roller coaster, and

Mike's stomach heaved each time they swooped sideways along the edge of a bank.

Reindeer Station was a small grouping of deserted houses on the bank of a channel of the Mackenzie River. The structures reminded Mike of pictures he'd seen of old houses in the Yukon during the gold rush. The houses were pretty plain but still stood out in contrast to the stark whiteness surrounding them.

Mike and his companions pitched in and gathered wood, which Victor used to start a fire in a clearing near the deserted houses. They pulled up some logs that others had employed for the same purpose, and Mike sat happily by the fire, sleepy and content. Donnie and Victor hunkered down to his right, with the girls on the other side of the flames. Mike didn't know if it was the heat from the fire or the fact that Mulluk was a safe distance away, but Donnie seemed pretty jubilant, too.

Victor extracted a Thermos from the sled and poured out steaming tea for everyone in cups he provided. Gingerly, Mike took a sip of the liquid and enjoyed the heat as the creamy, sweet substance slid down his throat. Victor went back to the sled and returned with saltines and canned meat, slicing up the latter and handing out portions to the group. Mike had never tasted anything so good in his life.

"So, Mike, what do you think of your first skidoo trip?" Victor asked.

"It's fantastic! I went out with friends a couple of times down south but never had a chance to drive. And we always drove across farm fields and stuff. It was nothing like this. I never thought I'd be driving on an ice road."

Everyone smiled and enjoyed their tea, slipping into comfortable silence.

Mike glanced at the old buildings behind them. "Victor, why are those buildings sitting empty like that? And if it's called Reindeer Station, where are all the reindeer?"

In the 1930s the Canadian government brought Laplanders from Scandinavia and reindeer from Alaska in order to raise a domesticated herd in the Northwest Territories, and this is where they settled. At that time Inuvik didn't exist."

"They tried to move people to Inuvik from Aklavik, right?" Mulluk interjected.

Victor nodded. "That's right. The Laplanders lived here and raised the reindeer. The idea was to sell the meat and make it into a type of industry for the area. Aklavik existed, but it's always had a problem with flooding in the springtime. It still does. It gets so bad at times that the streets disappear and people can only get around town by boat.

"That's when the government had another one of its bright ideas. There was a spot on the river not far from Reindeer Station that never flooded, so they decided they'd move the people from Aklavik to there. The new town was eventually called Inuvik. But there was a slight problem." Victor bit into a saltine.

"Nobody would move," Mulluk said, smirking.

"That's right. No one bothered to see if everyone would move for sure. Even though Inuvik didn't flood, most people refused to relocate from Aklavik. They were used to it, despite all the flooding. So, in the end, there were two towns — Inuvik and Aklavik. With Inuvik so close to Reindeer Station, the Laplanders decided to move there, too, which by then was larger and had more conveniences."

Mike nibbled on some meat and a saltine, then asked, "What happened to the reindeer?"

Victor smiled. "Selling them for a profit and creating a type of industry for the area didn't really work out. A family still owns the herd, but it's not the kind of thriving business the government hoped it would be."

"And now Reindeer Station's a ghost town," Mike said, studying the abandoned houses. "Let's see now, up here you've got Tuktoyaktuk, Aklavik, and Inuvik."

"Hey, don't forget Tsiigehtchic and Fort McPherson," Donnie chimed in.

"Sorry, I forgot," Mike said. "Tuktoyaktuk, Aklavik, Inuvik, Tsiigehtchic, and Fort McPherson, where Donnie's from."

Donnie nodded and smiled drowsily.

"Mike, do you play hockey?" Trish asked shyly. "What did you do for fun in Edmonton? I mean, St. Albert."

"I played a bit of hockey, but it wasn't my favourite thing to do. I mostly played lacrosse. My team won the provincial championships last year. Other than that I skied in the winter when we had time to go to the mountains and played most sports at school."

"He's amazing at basketball," Donnie said. "You should've seen him go up against Bobby Vittrekwa and Gwen Thrasher. He's likely the best player after Tommy Aleekuk."

Mike grinned sheepishly and stared at the fire.

Mulluk snorted. "I heard about you and Gwen. Everybody says it was love at first sight."

The girls all giggled. Even Donnie chuckled, holding his gloves up to his face. When Mike glanced up, Donnie quickly looked away, but Mike saw his shoulders shake with laughter and punched him lightly in the back.

"Lacrosse is an aboriginal sport," Victor said.

Mike's face lit up. "It's a great sport, Victor. It's like a combination of basketball and hockey, with lots of running. You can hit the other team or hammer them with your stick. And there's way more scoring than in hockey. You've got to be in shape, man, because you never stop running — just like soccer. And the hand-eye coordination you need is unbelievable."

"It's too bad no one plays it up here," Claudine said. "It sounds exciting."

Mike's enthusiasm withered as the full gravity of Claudine's words sank in. Somewhere at the back of his mind there had been a nagging, sickening feeling that lacrosse wasn't played in Inuvik. Now the reality was staring him in the face.

Victor placed a hand on Mike's shoulder. "I'm sorry, Mike. I can tell the game means a lot to you."

Mike shrugged and studied the fire gloomily. "I don't know if I can live without lacrosse. I don't know how my parents could do this to me. No one told me Inuvik didn't have lacrosse. This whole move was going to be a big adventure and I'd have plenty of fun, they told me."

"Mike, if your parents had told you Inuvik didn't have lacrosse, do you think it would've changed anything? Would it have made any of this easier?"

Mike shook his head but didn't look at Victor.

"I know it's hard, Mike, but you have to look for what isn't obvious. Look around you. Take your time. Something's waiting for you in Inuvik. Something you'll take with you for the rest of your life."

"Right now it's pretty hard to see anything," Mike said. "Today's pretty nice, but it's not lacrosse. As far as I'm concerned, all I can see is no lacrosse, a monster who wants to kill me, and a girl who plays sports like a boy and wants to beat the crap out of me."

Victor stared at Mike, baffled by his comments.

"He's talking about Joseph Kiktorak and Gwen Thrasher," Donnie said.

"Okay, I see. Mike, sometimes people aren't what they seem. Just like moving to Inuvik, you have to look deeper. Joseph and Gwen have good hearts, but they're angry at everything around them right now. Just like you. You don't know what their situation is, so be patient. Maybe they're part of the reason you're here."

Victor let his words sink in for a moment, then continued. "Gwen and Joseph are searching for something. Maybe you are, too, and you just don't know it. Maybe it's here in front of you. We never know what life will bring us, but if we take things with a smile on our faces, life looks a whole lot better. Right now Gwen and Joseph can't smile. They don't know who they are."

"I know who I am," Mike protested. "I'm a guy who loves lacrosse and misses St. Albert."

Victor frowned. "Mike, do you really know who you are? I don't think you do. You're an athletic boy who loves lacrosse. Lacrosse is a big part of you, and I don't think your time with the sport is done, but I sense you're so much more. The first day I met you I could feel your inner strength. I sense the warmth of your heart and how you accept others around you."

"Mike, your skin is dark," Victor said. "I'm curious. What's your heritage?"

"A mix of things, I guess. My dad's Irish. My mom's family is from South Africa. I think she's a mix of Zulu, German, and Filipina."

Victor raised an eyebrow. "You think? Why don't you know?"

"I never really stopped to figure it out, I guess."

Victor motioned in Mulluk's direction. "My granddaughter there is both Gwich'in and Inuvialuit. She embraces both of her cultures. She's part of the Inuvialuit group that travels and shows others our traditional dances. She knows who she is and she keeps our traditions alive. By acting out the stories and culture of our people through dance that has been part of us for many years, she finds herself. I think, Mike, you need to find yourself. You need to discover who you truly are."

"I don't need to know about my culture. I need to figure out what's going to happen to me right now."

"Mike, how do you know where you're going if you don't know where you came from?"

Sighing, Mike threw a stick into the fire.

Victor glanced at the sled. "It's getting dark. We better head for home."

CHAPTER 11

For the next week Mike left for school, came home, did homework, ate supper, and then went to his room. He never smiled or talked. He simply looked at the floor as if it could provide the answer.

At supper one night Ben asked his son what was wrong. Instead of answering, Mike looked at the floor as if there were a reply there. Finally, he glanced up at his mother, then focused his attention on his father. "Why didn't you tell me there was no lacrosse in Inuvik?"

"Mike, you know we had to make this move no matter what," Ben said. "You were upset from the very beginning. Telling you there was no lacrosse here would've made you even more disappointed. I tried to tell you a couple of times, but something always got in the way."

Ben cleared his throat, then continued. "I'm really sorry. I should've told you as soon as we found out. I guess in the end it didn't make things any easier. You'd think at my stage in life I'd know that the truth is the only way to go. I guess ... well, I guess I was having my own problems knowing there wasn't going to be a team for me to coach anymore."

"I think I understand, Dad. It must've been hard." He picked up his fork and started to eat the chili in front of him. Then he looked at his mother. "Mom?"

"Yes, Mike."

"What are we? I mean, what culture are we?"

"You pretty much know what I know. Grandma and Grandpa are from South Africa. Grandma's a mixture of Filipina and German, and Grandpa is Zulu and German. South Africa's a huge melting pot of nationalities and you're a result of all that melting."

"And I'm as Irish as Irish can be!" Ben said, grinning.

Mike almost scowled at his father, then asked his mother, "But what's our culture? What are some of our traditions?"

Jeannie wiped her mouth with a napkin. "Well, to be honest, Mike, I don't really know much about our culture or heritage. I was born in England, and we moved to Canada when I was really young."

"Have you ever tried to find out about your heritage? Surfed the Net? Talked to Grandma or Grandpa?"

Jeannie sighed. "I haven't really thought about it much, Mike. Grandma doesn't talk about the past a great deal … and, well, I haven't dug into things myself."

Mike turned his attention to his father. "Irish, eh?"

Ben squirmed, glanced at his wife, then burbled, "Faith and begorrah, laddie!"

Mike threw his napkin onto his plate angrily and stood up. "You guys don't know a thing! And it isn't funny! How can you sit there and joke about it when you don't know a thing? How do you know where you're going if you don't know where you came from?" Pushing his chair back hard, he stomped out of the dining room, ran up the stairs two at a time, and slammed the door to his bedroom.

For a long time Mike sat on his bed and stared at the wall. Things were so confusing. It hurt like crazy that he wasn't going to play lacrosse this year. But something inside him was fighting the hurt, and it didn't really seem as bad anymore. It had been so much fun going to Reindeer Station, and everyone had been so nice. Except for Gwen Thrasher and Joseph Kiktorak, things in Inuvik were kind of looking up a bit. He was getting to know some of the guys at school. Donnie was a geek, but he was a good friend and really funny to be around. Mike smiled to himself in the dark, then heard a bleep from the other side of the room.

Walking over to where his computer glowed dimly in the dark, he plopped into the swivel chair, wiggled the mouse across, and watched as the monitor brightened and the screen saver disappeared.

"SHOOTER has just signed in!"

Spencer! Their computers had been working for a few days now, but with everything else on his mind he hadn't bothered much with messages and stuff. Before supper he'd signed on to Instant Messenger and forgotten about it.

"SHOOTER says: Wassup, Mikey?"

"Nothing 2 much U?"

"SHOOTER says: School=[[and LAX=D."

"LAX already!"

"SHOOTER says: Spring camp at the garrison. You playing yet or busy building igloos=D."

Mike sat back and sighed. He'd forgotten that they'd be training already for the season. Spencer likely played winter lacrosse, too. Mike leaned forward and continued to type.

"I wish! No LAX here!"

"SHOOTER says: That sucks! No LAX at all?"

"No LAX but lots of fun snowmobiling! It's amazing"

Mike couldn't believe he'd just typed those words. But it was true. He really enjoyed being out with Victor. He leaned back again. Maybe it was being out with Victor and Donnie more than the snowmobiling. He stared at the ceiling. The computer bleeped.

"SHOOTER says: can't believe you not playing LAX! Your brain frozen! LOL"

"Ha-ha."

There was a soft knock at the door. Mike turned and saw his mother outlined in the doorway by the light in the hall.

"Can I come in, Mike?"

"I guess. I just have to sign off."

"Who are you talking to?"

"Spencer"

"G2G," Mike typed.

"SHOOTER says: OK bye."

Mike swivelled in the chair so he could face his mother as she sat on the bed.

"That's nice. What's Spencer up to?"

Mike kicked at the floor. "They started training for lacrosse already."

They both fell silent for a moment.

"Are you okay, Mike? I know the move's been hard on you, but it seemed as if you'd started feeling a little more at home. Then the last few days you were so quiet. Now tonight at supper ... You just seemed different about things. Is there anything you want to talk about?"

Mike fidgeted with his computer mouse. "I'm ... I'm pretty confused right now. I mean, I was so mad about lacrosse, and then all of a sudden I'm not mad. I had such a great time with Victor and Donnie and the girls the other day. It was so much fun to drive a snowmobile and be out with Victor. All my friends in St. Albert would say Donnie's a super geek. To me, though, he's a super guy, and real funny. And Victor's one of the nicest people I've ever met. When he talks, it's like he's ... I don't know, one of those sensei guys in the movies or something. He's kind and smart at the same time. Even though I was so upset about lacrosse and not being able to play anymore, he made me feel almost happy about it or something. He made it seem like if I really, truly, loved lacrosse, I'd play again someday, and it wasn't the end of the world." Mike stopped and stared at the swirls of the screen saver now moving across the luminous surface of the monitor.

"Victor does seem like a very nice man," Jeannie said. "In fact, everyone I've met in Inuvik seems great so far. This one lady I ran into at the post office told me that Victor's one of the most respected elders in Inuvik."

"Mom, Victor said that he felt I was in Inuvik to learn something. He said something that really started me thinking about people and life, and just, trying to understand everybody. He asked me how I knew where I was going if I didn't know where I came from. I hadn't ever thought of that before, and it's true. People up here learn about their heritage and language and stuff. I don't know anything about South Africa or Grandma or Grandpa. I guess I don't know really who I am inside. I don't know anything about those things. It seems kind of important now, though. Do you understand?"

Jeannie nodded. "I think I do, Mike. All your life you've played sports. You've always done well at school, but you've never stopped to wonder about yourself, your heritage, and the world around you. You know, tonight you made *me* realize I really haven't taken the time to figure out who I am, either." She smiled ruefully at her son. "I'm your mother and I'm Sergeant Watson's wife. But really, who am I? Mike, do you want me to call Grandma and ask her to write to you about what she knows, about your heritage and great-grandma and grandpa?"

"I think that would at least help, Mom. I don't think that's the only thing that's confusing right now, but I think what you're suggesting would help."

Jeannie walked over to Mike and ran her fingers through his dark, curly hair. "We'll figure things out, I'm sure." Bending over, she kissed him on the forehead, then headed for the door. Pausing in the doorway, she glanced back at her son. "I love you, Mike. I'll see you in the morning."

His mother was already halfway down the stairs to the main floor, when Mike whispered, "I love you. too, Mom."

CHAPTER 12

Even though Mike was confused, he had to admit things were looking up at school. Classes were good, he hadn't seen Joseph Kiktorak in days, and his run-ins with Gwen Thrasher had been pretty much limited to passing her in the hall and seeing her on the basket-ball court with intramurals. In fact, Mike's basketball team was doing so well that it was in second place behind Gwen's bunch.

One of the reasons for their success was Donnie. He was amazing. After watching Mike's games, he'd sit and dissect each and every play. He had a photographic memory. After school he'd sit with Mike and detail why in his mind certain plays hadn't worked. Most of the time he was right. Mike used the information to go over things with Tommy, Mitchell, Tyler, and the other guys before the next games. It made a huge difference, and Mike could tell Donnie felt pretty good when the guys started to treat him with a whole new level of respect.

Every game with Gwen's team was intense, and Mike noticed that when they played each other, the gym was consistently packed. Much to his relief there hadn't been a repeat of the shot to the ribs, but the games were still pretty physical. Gwen's team was big and used its size whenever possible. They had two giants — Billy Greenland and Mark Kikoak. Billy was tall, and Mark was incredibly strong.

The teams finally stood one point apart in the standings, and the next time they met each other the gym was full. They played in the last twenty-minute slot, and Mike noticed even the teachers ventured from the sanctuary of the staff lunch room and were standing along the back wall, waiting for the highly anticipated match.

Donnie discussed strategy with Mike the night before and ventured that the teams were virtually equal in talent. He figured the one advantage Mike and the guys had was their team play and their ability to stay level-headed. Gwen, Billy, and Mark were all emotional players. Most of the time their emotion worked to their advantage. But if the game was close, there were little things that Mike's team could do to throw Gwen and her guys off. When the game got late and if the score was tight, Donnie figured that was their ace in the hole.

Mike was warmed up and watched Gwen and her teammates go through drills around the basket. She hit every shot she attempted and looked as if she was in a perfect rhythm. Turning under the basket to retrieve a ball going toward the stands, she caught Mike's eye. For an instant the old familiar smoulder locked Mike in her gaze, but then her eyes seemed to soften and the beginning of a smile touched the corners of her mouth. It only lasted an instant before she whirled away and finger-rolled a shot up and into the net. Mike felt heat rise in his cheeks and realized he was holding his breath. Releasing the air from his lungs, he let it audibly blow past his lips before he rose to collect his thoughts.

"Tweeeeeet!" The referee blew his whistle. "Balls in! Let's go, guys!"

Mike's team huddled around Tommy and shouted, "One, two, three, *team*!"

Tommy hit the floor first, with Mike, Mitchell, Tyler, and David Elanik following.

The game was incredibly intense. At no point did either team have more than a two-basket lead. Gwen was guarding Mike so close that it was almost impossible to move. And for his part he returned the favour. They matched each other move for move, stride for stride, shot for shot. And once again it came down to the last shift in the last minute of the game. This time the score was tied.

Tyler made an incredible block on a drive to the net by Billy Greenland and turned the ball up the court, quickly passing off to David. David spotted Mike breaking for the net and lobbed a long, desperate pass. Mike turned back for the ball in full stride. He sensed Gwen beside him but focused on the ball as it arched over his head. Stretching for the ball in full stride, he watched as it cradled into his palms, while Gwen tried to slap it away. With one step Mike left his feet and flipped the ball at the net. Gwen rose at the same time, colliding with Mike as the ball left his hands. Mike and Gwen fell together as the ball circled the hoop and plunged through the net.

Stretching his arms forward, Mike cushioned his impact as much as possible, but still landed heavily on top of Gwen as they hit the floor. She gasped as the air was forced from her lungs. Lying still for an instant, Mike stared deeply into the two most incredibly beautiful brown almond-shaped eyes he had ever seen.

"Nice game, Gwen," he managed to croak. Then, hesitating ever so slightly, he closed his eyes and kissed her full on the mouth.

When he opened his eyes again, he was on his back with Gwen glowering over him, almond eyes blazing. The room seemed to spin out of control, and a circle of faces danced around his head. He saw Donnie in the stands, eyes bulging from their sockets, hands covering his mouth. Tommy was beside Gwen, smiling from ear to ear. Mitchell, Tyler, David, and the other players were all laughing so hard they were doubled over at the waist. With an angry *"Arrrrgh!"* Gwen turned and bolted from the gym.

Tommy stepped forward and stuck his hand out to Mike, helping him up off the floor. "That, my southern friend, was the most incredible thing I've ever seen in my life!"

Mike shook his head. "Oh, my God! The basket or the kiss?"

"Both!" Billy Greenland bellowed.

"You should've seen her face!" Tyler chirped.

Mike rolled his eyes. It was almost too much to stomach. "Oh, man! I have no idea why I did that. She's going to kill me. I just know it."

"Maybe. But I don't think so." Donnie huffed as he pushed his way past the other boys, chest heaving, trying to catch his breath. "When you kissed her, she closed her eyes, too. She got this really creepy smile on her face. Kind of like a zombie right before it takes a bite of human flesh. Then her face scrunched up like she bit into a chunk of muktuk left in the sun too long. And, man, was she ever mad. She smacked you across the face like Iron Man laying a licking on a super villain."

"Oh, crap!" Mike sighed and ran a hand through his hair.

Tommy slapped Mike on the back. "Look on the bright side, buddy. We're in first place, and I don't think you need to worry about Gwen guarding you that close ever again."

All of the boys laughed as they rumpled Mike's hair.

Word of the "kissing" incident spread like wildfire. Considering practically every student and teacher had witnessed the event, it didn't take much. Mike was beside himself. Now he was confused about every part of his life in Inuvik.

At school he dodged from class to class with his head down, avoiding eye contact with everyone. For their part the guys didn't let up. Every once in a while he'd hear a loud kissing sound in the hall. When he glanced up, Tommy, Mitchell, Tyler, or another one of the gang would be giggling and grinning from ear to ear. Thankfully, he didn't run into Gwen.

One day when he went to the store for his mom, he imagined everyone was whispering behind his back and that every smile was at his expense. He was scrunched down in one of the grocery aisles at the Northern Store searching for dill pickles when a firm hand gripped his shoulder. When he looked up, Victor was smiling down at him.

"Hey, Victor," he said.

"Considering all the use they're getting, your lips don't look chapped at all," Victor said.

Mike groaned. "Oh, no! Not you, too!"

Victor laughed and put his arm around Mike's shoulders as he stood up. "She's a pretty girl, and you're a handsome young man. I don't blame you. If I was a hundred years younger, I'd try to kiss her, too." He ruffled Mike's hair.

"It's not like that, Victor," Mike protested. "I don't know what came over me."

"So you don't think she's cute?"

"No!" Mike replied all too quickly. Victor raised an eyebrow, and Mike looked down sheepishly. "Okay. Yeah, I guess she's cute. Actually, I think she's beautiful.

Beautiful but mean … and she hates me! And she plays basketball like a boy. Why am I telling you this? And how do you know about it?"

"I have my sources, Mike. And don't be so sure she hates you. I bet she went home and kissed herself in the mirror just to pretend it was you all over again." Victor laughed so hard at his own joke that he began to cough. "I have to run, Mike, so take care of yourself. And don't get into any more trouble." He tapped Mike on the shoulder and began to walk away.

"Don't worry, Victor. I'll be careful."

The biggest surprise came when Donnie called Mike one day after school. "Mike you gotta get over here quick!"

"Over where, Donnie? Slow down."

"Back at school, man. Go to the gym. You're not gonna believe this."

"Believe what?"

"Look, I can't explain. Just get over here."

"Donnie, I have homework and —" The phone clicked dead on the other end.

Hurriedly, Mike pulled on his boots and threw on his parka as he ran out the door. Bolting down the steps, he turned and ran up the street to the light. As usual it was red, but he timed his stride to race across between trucks as they passed on the street. Out of breath, he reached the school doors and pushed through. The halls were deserted, and after pulling off his boots, he scampered down the slippery tiles as fast as his stocking feet would let him.

As he approached the big double doors to the gym, he didn't hear a sound. Usually, there were muffled shouts, the squeak of runners, or the thud of balls bouncing on the floor if anything was happening inside. Slowing to a walk, Mike pushed open the doors and quickly stepped inside.

He spotted Donnie alone under the basketball hoop at one end of the gym. The big kid was smiling ear to ear, eyes huge behind his glasses. He was standing in front of something and hiding his hands behind his back. As Mike got closer, Donnie held up two identical objects.

The lacrosse net behind Donnie was a homemade version someone had put together in a welding shop. All the same it looked sturdy and perfect in dimension. Mike recognized the lacrosse sticks Donnie held proudly in the air. They were both his. When Mike reached the net, he placed a hand on its crossbar and asked, "Donnie, what's all this?"

"Well, I kind of got talking to your dad after your thing with Gwen." Donnie paused as Mike rolled his eyes and shook his head. "It wasn't about that!" His eyes grew large and serious. "It was about you being confused, and how the whole thing with Gwen made stuff even worse. I asked him what you did in St. Albert to make yourself feel better when you were upset or what you did to relax. He said you always went to the garage or outside and shot the lacrosse ball at the net. He said it always helped you think and made you feel better.

"So your dad went to Pete's Welding and had this net made up. It kind of looks weird if you ask me with the point at the back instead of round like a hockey net, but your dad says it's the right way, and I'm no expert. I went on the Internet, and sure enough, this is the way it should be. I didn't have time to paint it red or anything, but the grey metal doesn't look too bad."

When Mike remained silent, Donnie nervously continued. "Then I went to Mr. Koe to see if he'd let us come in here after hours. He said, sure, as long as it isn't scheduled for anyone else. So today it wasn't scheduled for someone else. Your dad brought the net over in his truck, and we lugged it in." Donnie shrugged, raising his hands above his head. "As you know, the sticks, well, they're your sticks. Man, they've gotta be the strangest things I've ever seen. And this ball is hard as a rock." Donnie held out a white Indian rubber lacrosse ball.

Mike reached out and gently took one of the sticks from Donnie. He fondly looked it up and down as he balanced it in his hands. "Donnie, you've got to be just about the best friend I've ever had. And I've had a lot of friends."

Donnie's chubby cheeks turned pinkish-brown. "You *are* the best friend I've ever had, Mike. But I haven't had many friends, really."

Mike took the ball from Donnie's hand and placed it in the basket at the end of the composite stick. "Donnie, you'd have a lot of friends, but you scare people with that big brain of yours. If people took their time and got to know you, they'd see you're just about one of the coolest guys around. And one of the funniest, too."

Donnie looked up and smiled. "Really?"

"Really, Donnie. And you watch. More and more people are going to realize that and someday you're going to have more friends than you'll know what to do with." Mike cradled the ball in the basket of the stick. "Now let's stop all this male bonding crap and shoot the ball around."

Mike jogged in a circle away from the net as Donnie backed off. Stopping, Mike drew the stick back, took a step forward, and whipped the ball into the top corner of the net.

"Holy crap!" Donnie cried. "Does that ball ever fly!"

"I was taking it easy on that one because I haven't held a stick in months. The ball can rocket over a hundred and sixty kilometres per hour easy. It's the fastest game on two feet."

Mike scooped the ball out of the net, jogged away once again, stopped, whirled, and this time fired a shot underhanded with the same result. *Whooosh!* Into the other top corner.

Donnie gasped. "Man, I wouldn't want to be a goalie. That ball could kill a guy!"

"I wouldn't want to be a goalie, either." Mike retrieved the ball once more. "The ball can come at you from almost any angle. In hockey the shots all come up off the ice for the most part. In lacrosse they can come overhand, underhand, sideways, or as bounce shots. The net's smaller than a hockey net, but that doesn't keep a heap of goals from getting scored. In lacrosse an average game is likely, oh, I don't know, maybe 13–12. Here, you take a turn."

Mike tossed the ball to Donnie. He awkwardly batted at the ball with the lacrosse stick, sending it bouncing and skidding off to the side of the gym. Laughing, Mike chased after it and deftly scooped it into the basket of his stick.

"You can't fight the ball, Donnie. You don't need to swat at it. Hold the stick out with the head and mesh facing me. I'm going to bounce the ball over. Just move the stick in front of the ball and let it hit the mesh. When you feel it hit the mesh and go into the pocket, just turn the stick sideways. Okay?"

Donnie nodded and stood with his legs wide apart, arms stiffly holding the stick off to the side and slightly in front. Mike bounced the ball in Donnie's direction. Given their distance apart, the ball took a second bounce and shot at Donnie with unexpected velocity. He cried and jumped out of the way. Mike burst out laughing, bending over with his stick across his thighs.

"Holy crap, what was that?" Donnie said. "It bounced normal and then shot out like a rocket."

Mike couldn't answer right away. He was laughing too hard. Wiping his eyes, he straightened. "That always catches people, Donnie. The ball is Indian rubber, no pun intended. When it bounces, every second bounce takes off like that. Watch this."

Backing farther away, Mike bounced the ball toward the net. Sure enough, the bounces were interspersed.

One bounce ahead, the next bounce slower, one bounce ahead, the next bounce slower, and so on.

Donnie shook his head. "It's almost like every second bounce has some kind of spin on it."

Mike nodded. "Okay, let's try it again, Donnie."

Donnie spread his legs once more. Holding the stick stiffly forward and to the side, he peered through the thick lenses of his glasses. Mike bounced the ball, and this time Donnie was ready for the funny hop. He quickly shifted his stick in front of the ball, and as the sphere hit the pocket, he turned it upward. The ball stayed in!

"Way to go!" Mike shouted.

Donnie smiled broadly. "Let's do that again, Mike."

"Okay, Donnie, but that was beginner's luck. It's going to get harder, because I'm going to make you move for the ball, not just stand still."

"Jeez, Mike! Take it easy. Do I look like a lacrosse player? Don't answer that. Just take it easy."

Mike laughed. "Okay. Throw the ball back."

Donnie looked at the ball in the pocket of his stick. Slowly, he lifted the stick, drew it back over his head, and made a throwing motion. Shock registered on his face when there was no sign of the ball leaving the stick. Mike doubled over and began to laugh again, pointing at Donnie. Bewildered, Donnie glanced from side to side. Turning, he spotted the ball bouncing on the floor directly behind him. "Let me guess," he said. "It fell out of the stick when I had it back behind my head ready to shoot?"

"That would be absolutely correct, Mr. *Dee-basteeeeyen!*"

Donnie walked over and tried to slide the head of the stick under the ball to scoop it up. It skittered away across the floor. Smiling sheepishly, he lumbered across the floor as fast as his heavy legs could carry him.

During the next hour, Mike laughed harder than he could remember doing in a long time. Donnie, for his part, laughed between all the huffing, puffing, and grunting as he tried to master basic lacrosse skills that Mike made look so easy. The rest of the time he gasped in amazement as Mike filled the net with shots behind his back, between his legs, and from weird angles around the gym.

The boys finally sat on the floor beside the net. Mike had worked up a bit of a sweat running after balls that Donnie couldn't get to. It felt good, and he smiled over at Donnie, who looked as if he were about to die. The big boy was stretched out on his back, belly heaving in the air. Sweat shone in his spiky bristle of black hair. His cheeks were a dark rosy red, and perspiration beaded his forehead above his glasses.

"You gonna live, Donnie?"

Donnie glared at Mike. "Oh, God, I don't think so. I think I might be having a heart attack or a stroke."

Mike started to laugh and flopped on his back, lying flat on the floor. He stared at the banks of fluorescent lights on the ceiling for a moment. "You know, Donnie. I do feel better. Even though I can't play, just tossing the ball around makes me feel better. Do you think Mr. Koe would let us come here every day after school?"

"Every day?" Donnie croaked, concern filling his eyes.

"Well, not every day, but a few days a week. I mean, if the gym's busy, we can't, but it would be nice to come and toss the ball around. You started to get better near the end there, and soon enough, you'll be catching and throwing as well as me."

Donnie lifted his head. "Do you really think so?"

"Not really. You're actually pretty terrible. But you'll get better."

Donnie grimaced at Mike and playfully threw his stick. Mike rolled out of the way and chuckled.

Something caught Mike's attention at the door to the gym. Turning quickly, he spotted someone ducking out of sight as the door slowly closed. "Did you see who that was, Donnie?" Mike asked as he jumped to his feet.

Donnie raised his head off the floor. "What?"

Mike ran to the door and quickly jerked it open just in time to see someone disappear around the corner at the end of the hall. There was no mistaking who it was. Mike went back inside the gym and plunked down beside Donnie.

"Well?" Donnie asked, sitting up. "Was there really someone, or was it your imagination?"

"It was Gwen Thrasher," Mike said quietly.

Donnie's eyes popped.

That night at supper Mike smiled and talked in a way he hadn't really done since moving to Inuvik. Then, just before he and his parents started dessert, he put down his fork and turned to his father. "Thanks, Dad. I had a lot of fun with Donnie at the gym today."

Ben held up his hand in protest. "It was Donnie's idea. You didn't kill the big fellow, did you?"

"Almost but not quite. He's awful, but he's a lot of fun and a real nice guy." Mike glanced at the clock above the fridge. "Oh, man, I almost forgot! It's Thursday. The Rush are playing at home to Philadelphia, and I bet I can pick it up on the radio. Good night, you guys." Jumping up, Mike pecked his mother on the cheek and ran upstairs.

As soon he was in his bedroom, Mike carefully turned the radio on and scrolled through the channels, once again hitting broadcast after broadcast from around the world. Suddenly, he stopped. This was it — the broadcast from Rexall Place in Edmonton. The second quarter had already started, and the Rush were up 5–3. They were having a great season and were a sure thing to make the playoffs. Mike listened intently as the action moved back and forth between the two teams. *"Yaaaa!"* he cried, pumping his fist in the air as Jimmy Quinlan, his favourite player, took a pass in front of the net and popped another one in for the Rush.

Lying back on his pillow, he placed both hands under his head and listened intently as the Wings won the faceoff and turned the ball toward the Rush's end. They set up in the Rush's zone and moved the ball around the perimeter, attempting to set up a scoring opportunity. Mike pictured the interior of the arena and the crowd as it held its breath, hoping the Rush's defence would hold. The announcer screamed wildly as the Rush's goalie made an amazing save and kicked the ball out in spectacular fashion. Who would have ever guessed that he would enjoy listening to something on the radio more than watching a program on television downstairs? Soon, though, his eyes became heavy and closed.

ROBERT FEAGAN

Visions of the Rush floated through his mind, replaced by a beautiful set of stormy, almond-shaped eyes. The last vision he had before drifting off was of Donnie lying on the gym floor, stomach thrust into the air. Mike smiled in the dark and fell fast asleep.

CHAPTER 13

Life seemed pretty good. Donnie and Mike were at the gym pretty much every day after school. Mike could drive the Polaris on his own now, and on days they didn't shoot the lacrosse ball around, the two friends drove out onto the river or had fun zipping up and around a steep hill near town called Old Baldy. The days were longer, the sun was stronger, and the air was warmer.

Victor took Mike and Donnie to his camp several times on weekends. The camp was about sixty-six kilometres northwest of Inuvik. Like Reindeer Station, it was about a two-hour trip each way by snowmobile, and they were lucky enough to stay overnight on a couple of occasions. The camp was at the confluence of the Axel Channel and the Mackenzie River on the delta side. Victor had an eight-metre-by-eight-metre house there with a loft. For heat there was a two-hundred-litre stove. Mike loved the feeling of waking up, warm and toasty in his sleeping bag, his breath visible in the chilly air of the house. Victor would start a fire in the stove, and the warm, smoky smell would rapidly spread throughout the cabin.

Victor explained to Mike how the connection between the land and the Inuvialuit and Gwich'in people was so strong and important. Most people had jobs in town now, but any time they could spend at camp or on the land were the happiest moments in their lives.

Mike was beginning to understand. Victor was one of the nicest people he knew. And when they went to the camp, he saw Victor change. His smile was bigger, he was more relaxed, and he seemed to have an understanding of everything around him. The strange thing was that Mike felt as if he was starting to experience the same things. Every time he went to the camp he experienced an inner peace or calm he couldn't explain. All his problems seemed a little smaller, every dream was a little closer, and every smile appeared a little warmer. Some of his happiest moments were talking with Victor and Donnie around the stove, or standing beside their snowmobiles when they took a break on the trip to or from Inuvik.

It had been a slow process, but the guys at school were treating him like one of the gang now, too. He still spent most of his time with Donnie, but he hung out a bit with Tommy, Mitchell, and Bobby Vittrekwa. It was spring, and the local hockey league had started playoffs. Most of the guys played, and Mike and Donnie went to the arena to watch.

One of the big semifinal games was on, and Mike and Donnie didn't want to miss it. Tyler Snowshoe and Tommy were on the same team. They were two of the best players in town, and everyone figured they were the favourites to win the league championship. In most small towns everybody turned out for sporting events, and Inuvik was no exception. The arena at the family centre was packed as Donnie and Mike waded in to find a place to stand and watch the game.

The action was fantastic, with lots of wide-open, end-to-end offence. Although Mike's first love was lacrosse, he was a decent hockey player and found himself thinking about the next season and getting on one of the local teams. He wouldn't be the best, but he could tell by the play on the ice that he would hold his own. In lacrosse he was all offence, but in hockey defence was his strength. With so many offensively strong players, he would likely prove valuable to one of the teams.

Tommy and Tyler's team won 8–5, and Donnie and Mike goofed around as the crowd cleared, waiting to see their buddies when they came out of the dressing room. Donnie grabbed Mike's toque and threatened to throw it. Mike shifted from side to side, attempting to block Donnie's throw. Donnie finally tossed the hat to the left, and Mike leaped without looking. With a thud he hit one of the people standing to the side and fell to the floor.

"Man, I'm sorry!" he said as he got to his feet.

"My buddy and I were just —" He stopped in mid sentence. For the second time in his brief existence in Inuvik, he was met with the cold stare of Joseph Kiktorak. The huge kid stepped in close and gave Mike a hard shove to the chest with both hands. Mike stumbled backward and collided with the concrete wall. Joseph followed in close and trapped him there, his left hand pinning Mike to the wall. All Mike could do was try to protect himself. He could see the scar on Joseph's left cheek standing out under the florescent light, and a hateful smirk twisted the corners of the boy's mouth.

"You think you're something else, don't you? You move into town and walk around like you own the place and everybody has to get out of your way. Well I'm not going to get out of your way."

It was the first time Mike had heard Joseph speak.

His voice was deep and mature for his age. Everything about him was mature for his age — his height, size, voice, and strength, from what Mike could feel through the hand pressing against his chest.

"No, I don't," Mike squeaked. "It was an accident. Donnie threw my hat, and I was only trying to catch it. I —"

"Oh, so you have to blame butterball over there. You can't even handle your own problems like a man. Well, you and your fat friend can go to hell!"

Mike felt anger heat his face. He quickly pulled his right arm upward and batted Joseph's hand away from his chest. "His name's Donnie. And he isn't my friend. He's my best friend. I don't think I'm better than anyone else, and I can fight my own battles. You're big and you think you're tough. Maybe you are. And maybe you'll kick the crap out of me. But I'll fight you right here and now if you want."

Joseph took a step back in surprise that quickly turned to resignation. "You're not worth it!" He glanced at Donnie and the rest of the crowd that had gathered around the two boys. "None of you are worth it!" He pushed past the few people who didn't get out of his way quickly enough and stomped off to the exit.

Donnie walked over to Mike as the rest of the crowd melted away.

"Man, what's wrong with that guy?" Mike asked. "It was an accident."

"He's always mad, Mike. I'm surprised he was here watching the hockey. It likely put him in an even worse mood."

"What do you mean?"

"Well, Joseph's a pretty incredible hockey player. He's fast, has size, and is unbelievably smart on the ice. Scouts from down south came and watched him all the time. Everybody figured he was going to be drafted by the Western Hockey League for sure. Then he got caught smoking pot, got kicked out of the league, and wasn't allowed back. On top of that, he had to live with his granny when his mom moved to Cambridge Bay. It was too much at the same time, and he's been one bitter, mean dude ever since!"

"Jeez, that's pretty rough. I mean, it's bad he was smoking pot and everything, but I don't know what I'd do if I got kicked out of lacrosse." Mike and Donnie fell silent, both realizing what Mike had said. "I guess in a way I have been kicked out of lacrosse, so I understand why he's mad. But —" he grinned at Donnie "— having good friends helps."

CHAPTER 14

It wasn't the same as playing, but Mike found being able to hold a lacrosse stick and shoot a ball around did make him feel better. That and his trips and talks with Victor were the things he looked forward to the most. The excursions with Victor were becoming more frequent as the spring weather continued to improve and daylight lasted longer. His dad even went on a few trips when he had the time.

Hanging out with Donnie was fun, too. It made Mike smile every time he pictured Donnie's eyes bugging out about something. Donnie was still pretty terrible at lacrosse, but he was catching the ball more consistently. He always seemed to get in the way of the ball, even when he should be getting out of the way.

Mike called him an Indian rubber magnet!

Most days after school the gym was deserted. Mike would run home, drop his books off, grab the lacrosse sticks, and race back to school where Donnie would be waiting. Mike and Donnie usually had the gym to themselves to shoot and laugh their heads off. It was their special time. It was for that reason that one day when Donnie and Mike heard voices coming from the gym as they approached that Mike felt a surprising anger rise in his chest. What jerks had the nerve to steal their time in the gym?

Mike pushed one of the heavy doors open with such ferocity that it smacked loudly against the wall before rebounding violently back into his shoulder. He stood in the doorway gathering his senses as he surveyed the faces staring at him. Tommy Aleekuk and David Elanik waved at him from across the gym. He limply waved back and tried to figure out what was going on. It was some of the strangest stuff he'd ever seen.

"Oh, darn! They're having an Arctic Sports practice!" Mike had completely forgotten that Donnie was right behind him. Glancing back, he quickly turned once again to study the spectacle.

David, Tommy, and Mark Kikoak were there, as well as several guys he recognized but whose names he couldn't remember. There were girls, too. He watched in amazement as Gwen Thrasher took a short run, jumped straight into the air, and kicked a little fuzzy thing hanging from what appeared to be an aluminum pole.

Tommy jogged across the gym and gripped Mike in a handshake. "Hey, man, you come to try out for Arctic Sports?"

"I didn't even know there was such a thing," Mike said. "Donnie and I came to shoot the lacrosse ball around."

"That's what those crazy-looking things are?" Tommy nodded at the sticks in Mike's hand. "We're mostly down at this end, so if you guys want to bounce the ball around there, you can."

"Sure," Mike said. "We'll be careful and pass across the gym. Can we watch you guys for a bit first?"

Tommy grinned. "Hey, anybody can watch. You can even try if you're brave enough. Come on over!" He jogged back over to a group of guys standing in a huddle.

"Let's take a look, Donnie."

"It's pretty cool, Mike. These are sports the Inuit and Inuvialuit have been doing for hundreds of years. Most are pretty hard, too. It looks like they're going to do the airplane. If you're lucky, Mark will take a turn. He's one of the best around. I think he won a medal a couple of years ago at the Arctic Winter Games in Whitehorse."

Mike followed Donnie over. When they got there, David and Mark gave Mike a friendly "Hey," while the other guys nodded and smiled. Sure enough, it looked as if Mark was going to take a turn at something that appeared pretty freaky to Mike.

Mark lay on the floor face down. His arms were straight out from his sides at right angles, and his legs and feet were together, straight along the floor. David stood on the left side of Mark, Tommy on the right. They placed their hands under each of Mark's balled-up fists. Two other guys stood by Mark's feet, each putting their hands between a foot and the floor.

All at once Mark seemed to stiffen his entire body. "Ready!" he rasped between clenched teeth. The four boys lifted Mark at the same time, stopping with his body about a metre off the floor.

Mike gasped. "Holy crap!"

"That's the airplane," Donnie whispered. "Now they have to see how far he can stay like that." Mike watched as the four boys carried Mark slowly around the perimeter of the gym. He held his body perfectly rigid. Without realizing it Mike held his breath. Mark seemed to go forever. It was amazing! At last Mike could see Mark begin to tremble. He was fighting with everything he had, his face turning red, then purple. Finally, with a sigh, he collapsed on the floor.

"Phewwwww!" Mike exhaled. "That was one of the most incredible things I've ever seen."

Mark sat up on the floor and wiped the perspiration off his forehead. "You ready for a turn, South Boy?"

Mike smiled nervously. "Man, I don't know … That's got to be one of the most incredible things I've ever seen. I doubt if I could even make it off the floor."

Mark laughed. "Well, my man, there's only one way to find out."

"Go ahead, Mike," Donnie said. "I bet you can do it."

"Come on, Mike," the other boys urged. "Give it a shot."

Shaking his head, Mike knelt on the floor. "Mark, if I rip myself in half, I'm going to blame you."

Mark patted Mike on the shoulder. "Well, whatever you do, you better make it look good." He looked past Mike and motioned in that direction with his head.

Mike turned to find the rest of the group in the gym had gathered to watch. "Oh, God!"

Donnie caught his eye and nodded, urging Mike on.

"Here goes nothin'." Mike lowered himself and lay face down on the floor. Deliberately, he stuck his arms out from his sides at right angles and placed his feet together. Tommy moved to one side while David made his way to the other. Mark and another boy took their places by Mike's feet. Glancing upward, Mike spied Gwen standing partly obscured behind the circle of faces. Her expression was passive and betrayed nothing but interest.

Lying face down, Mike closed his eyes and tensed every muscle in his body. "Okay!" he breathed. Slowly, the four boys began to lift. Mike could feel pressure on his chest and stomach. It felt as if he were going to tear in half. The boys continued to lift until Mike was about a half metre off the floor. He began to tremble as they moved slowly ahead until finally he collapsed with a sigh.

"All right!" Tommy shouted, patting Mike on the back as he rolled over and sat up. There was scattered clapping and a few whoops from the group standing around. Donnie was smiling, wide-eyed, as he applauded furiously.

"That was great, Mike," Mark said. "Most people don't even get off the floor the first time they try. You're built like Tommy and me. Thick and thick! You're an airplane expert just waiting to happen."

Tommy and the other guys laughed.

The group scattered and continued to practise the different events. Mike stood and rubbed his chest.

"Hey," Tommy said, "your girlfriend's about to do the high kick. Watch this. She's really good, but, hey, I'm amazing."

Mike gave Tommy a playful shove and turned to watch. Gwen was alternately lifting her knees as high as possible as she warmed up.

"What exactly is she supposed to do?" Mike asked Tommy.

"Well, see that little toy seal hanging in the air from that pole?"

Mike nodded.

"Gwen has to jump in the air and kick it with one of her feet. The trick is, she has to land back on that same foot and regain her balance. If she lands on the other foot or loses her balance and puts the other foot down, it doesn't count."

"You've got to be kidding?" Mike murmured. "That toy seal's higher than her head."

"Just watch."

Gwen walked up to the little seal and gazed at it intently. It was as if she were staring it down or trying to intimidate it. The seal was suspended slightly higher than her head. Slowly, she backed away and stopped. She started to rock back and forth, and the muscles in her calves balled up and relaxed. Suddenly, she jogged forward and exploded upward, kicking as she lifted off.

The toes of her right foot extended above her head, striking the seal and sending it spinning upward before she landed expertly back on her right foot. Holding her arms out at her sides, she stabilized herself on her right foot and gained control before she lowered her left foot to the ground.

"Unbelievable," Mike said.

"Your girl's quite the athlete," Tommy whispered in his ear. "I bet she was thinking about that kiss right before she jumped." Mike punched Tommy in the arm, and Tommy grabbed him around the neck. They jostled for a moment or two before they settled down and laughed at each other.

"Let me try that lacrosse racket," Tommy said, pointing at Donnie, who was still holding both sticks.

Mike moaned. "They're called sticks. Just like hockey sticks. If you call them rackets again, I might have to beat you up a second time."

Tommy snorted. "You beat me up? I almost killed you back there." They bumped each other repeatedly as they hustled to the far end of the gym with Donnie. When they got there, Mike and Donnie dragged the net out of the storage room and set it up under the basket.

"Now that's one strange, ugly-looking net," Tommy said. "It looks even stranger than the rackets."

Mike scooped up the ball and ran away from the net. Turning, he fired the ball overhand without hesitation. It ripped into the top left corner of the net.

"Jeez!" Tommy gasped. "Give me that stick, Donnie." Donnie handed Tommy the other stick. He held it in his hands, pushed his fist into the pocket of the mesh, then held it up facing Mike.

"Pass the ball, Mike. Let me take a shot."

Mike lightly tossed the ball, but instead of catching it, Tommy swatted it just as Donnie had his first day. The ball bounced across the floor and back at the pocket of the stick.

"Okay, I guess it's harder than it looks," Tommy said.

Mike retrieved the ball and instructed Tommy to let the stick give as the ball hit the pocket. This time he caught it easily.

"Oh, yeah!" Tommy yelled. Turning, he reared back and fired the ball. It sailed straight out of the stick and hit the roof of the gym. The surprise on his face was priceless. "Okay, okay, so I need some practice. Toss it here again."

Tommy was determined, and over the next few minutes he had Mike pass him ball after ball. Each time his shots were visibly better. Soon he was hitting the net every time. He was a natural athlete.

"You're looking good, Tommy," Mike said. "You'll get better in no time. Here, let me show you a few things."

Tommy passed the ball, and without stopping, Mike shot in quick stick fashion as the ball hit the pocket of his stick. It sunk into the net. Tommy shook his head. Scooping the ball out of the net, Mike fired it in once more from behind his back, then underhand, and finally side arm.

"Okay, Tommy, try to take it away," Mike challenged.

Tommy grinned and moved in front of Mike. He swatted hard at Mike's stick, but Mike quickly swung it over his shoulder and then off to the side. It was as if the ball were glued in the pocket. Soon everyone in the gym had gathered around and was watching with interest.

It was no use. Even when Tommy managed to strike Mike's stick, Mike maintained control by cradling the ball. Then Mike passed Tommy the ball and quickly made him lose it or swatted it out of his stick. Soon some of the other boys wanted to try, and the sticks and ball were handed around as everyone had a turn.

"Hey, Gwen, do you want to give it a shot?" Mike asked.

Caught off guard by Mike's question, Gwen flushed. She hesitated to turn away, then stopped. "No thanks, Mike." She didn't smile, but she didn't frown, either. "You did better at the airplane than most people when they try it the first time."

Mike opened his mouth, but no words came out. Donnie was laughing over Gwen's shoulder. She turned quickly, gathered her things, and left the gym. Feeling a hand on his right shoulder, then on his left, Mike turned to see Tommy and David standing on either side of him.

"Isn't young love just wonderful, David?" Tommy asked.

"It sure is, Tommy. I think Mike and his woman should go on a date. I don't think she's called any of us by our first names in years. Hmm ... Gwen Watson. It does have a nice ring."

That night Mike lay in his dark bedroom, hands supporting the back of his head, eyes focused on the posters on the walls. He didn't really see them. Instead he replayed the events of the day in his mind. The Arctic Sports were awesome, and Tommy, David, Mark, and Gwen were all unbelievable athletes.

Gwen. A queasy warmth rippled through his stomach. He touched his cheeks. The heat had risen and settled there. Gwen had actually talked to him today.

It was fleeting, but she did say something nice. Mike rolled over, reached for the shortwave radio, turned it on, and scrolled through the channels. Even though he couldn't understand a word, he liked to stop for a few seconds to listen to some of the different languages he ran across. The sports were unbelievable, too: hockey, basketball, soccer, and of course lacrosse. After briefly listening to a few games that were underway, he found what he was looking for.

The Toronto Rock were playing the Buffalo Bandits in the Air Canada Centre. John Tavares played for Buffalo. He was a terrific forward and was the NLL's leading scorer of all time. Mike listened intently as he absorbed the flow of the game. Tavares scored, and Mike shook his head. When he listened to lacrosse games on radio, he seemed to feel the matches more than he did when he watched them on television. He didn't tell people that because he didn't think they would understand. Closing his eyes, he sank back into the intensity of the game, a grin on his face.

On the day the amazing thing happened, Mike, Donnie, and Mark played against Tommy, David, and another boy named Dennis Selamio. Mike was standing farthest away from the net when Donnie trapped a loose ball beside the net. He yelled at Donnie to pass the ball out so they could set things up. Donnie tried to lob the ball to Mike, but Tommy intercepted the pass. After briefly hesitating, Tommy hurtled toward Donnie and the net. Donnie's eyes grew huge behind his glasses, then narrowed in determination. He set his feet wide apart, bent low, and held his stick out in front, ready to bump Tommy off the ball. Donnie was too stationary, though, and Mike knew all Tommy had to do was make a quick move to blow past him before passing the ball.

Tommy was at full speed, charging straight for Donnie. Mike tensed as he realized Tommy had no intention of deking around Donnie. He was too close, and a head-on collision was inevitable. Donnie closed his eyes and prepared for the impact. As if in slow motion, Tommy pushed off with his muscular thighs and left his feet. Lifting himself into a tuck, he narrowly cleared Donnie's head and landed in a full run on the other side. When he pulled up beside the net, he turned and laughed.

Donnie stood facing away from the net, eyes tightly closed, stick held at arm's length in front of him. As laughter erupted around him, he opened his eyes and squinted. Turning slowly, he spotted Tommy doubled over, still laughing beside the net. "You jumped right over my head, didn't you?"

"I sure did," Tommy said. "Cleared your brush cut by, oh, maybe a millimetre."

"You could've taken my head off!"

Tommy, who had stopped laughing for a moment, broke out again in laughter so hard that he fell on his butt and rolled around.

When Donnie realized everybody else was sniggering, chuckling, or tittering, including Mike, he wailed, "It's not funny!"

Mike started to feel bad and walked over to his friend. "Donnie, I wasn't laughing at you. I've just never seen anything so incredible in my life. What Tommy did would be amazing to see in a real game. Can you imagine?"

"Yeah, actually, I can. I just lived through it, if you didn't notice."

Tommy approached the two. "I'm really sorry, Donnie You're a good sport. I promise I won't do it again. When a friend tells me not to do something, I stop."

Donnie glanced at Mike, then back at Tommy. "Well, I guess it's okay, Tommy. I know you weren't trying to hurt me or anything."

Mike shook his head. "That was awesome! My buddies in St. Albert would never believe something like that could happen."

Tommy seemed a little embarrassed. "Hey, Mike, I was just fooling around. I have to go now, but we'll catch you tomorrow. This lacrosse stuff is actually a lot of fun."

"Tommy," Mike said, "do you think you and Donnie and some of the guys would like to come over sometime and watch lacrosse DVDs? I've got some from NLL games that show some pretty mind-boggling stuff. It might be fun."

"I'd like that," Tommy said. "See you guys later." He turned and jogged away.

Mike focused his attention on Donnie. "You up for that, too, Donnie?"

Donnie was staring after Tommy and didn't seem to hear Mike.

"Earth to Donnie," Mike said, grinning.

Donnie finally came out of his trance. "Tommy said I was his friend. None of these guys have called me their friend before. They hardly ever talk to me."

"I told you, Donnie. All it takes is for people to get to know you. Then they realize what a great guy you are. Let's get out of here I've got a pile of homework to do."

CHAPTER 16

Boys, bags of chips, and bottles of pop were scattered everywhere in the living room of the Watson home when Ben walked in one night after work. As soon as Mike spotted his father, he got up from the DVD player and grinned. "Hey, Dad!"

The room became quiet as all the boys glanced at Ben.

"Hey, Mr. W!" Donnie chirped.

"Hey, yourself, Donnie," Ben said.

Mike motioned at his father. "Guys, this is my dad."

"Hey, everybody," Ben said, waving.

There was a rumbling of hellos and some waves as the boys shyly acknowledged Ben.

"You guys make yourselves at home," Ben said as he threaded his way through the bodies to get to the stairs. "I'm heading up to change out of my uniform. I'll see you in a bit."

When Ben returned downstairs, he took a chair from the kitchen and joined the boys, who were watching a portion of a DVD where all the big lacrosse hits were being shown.

"Jeez!" David Elanik cried. "They can't do that. That guy wound up and gave the other guy a two-handed chop."

"Oh, yes, they can," Mike said. "In lacrosse you can cross-check, and as long as it isn't too vicious, they let you hammer a guy like that."

"You're kidding, right?" Mark Kikoak said.

"I'm not kidding. Ask my dad. You can cross-check or body-check. Either way."

Everybody turned toward Ben, who cleared his throat. "Well, you guys are watching the National Lacrosse League. They let a little more go at that level than at the level you boys would play. But you'd still be able to cross-check, hit, and chop each other a bit like you see on TV."

"*Oh!*" the boys shouted collectively as two players sandwiched each other at full speed, sending their sticks into the air as they fell heavily to the floor.

"Oh, man, I'd love to play this game," Mark said. "It's even rougher than hockey."

"That might seem to be the case," Donnie said to everyone's surprise. "However, statistically there are far fewer injuries in lacrosse than hockey. This might interest you guys, too. I've been surfing the Net. Lacrosse was our only national sport before they officially added hockey. It was invented by aboriginal peoples, and one game could last for days. It was like a big game and party all at the same time. Box lacrosse came later, and though it looks rough, more guys get hurt bad in hockey and football. Most of the injuries in lacrosse are smaller stuff. Right now it's one of the fastest-growing sports in the world."

The room was silent for a moment, then Tommy shouted, "Oh, my God! Did you see that!"

Everyone's attention was on the television again. Donnie looked around sheepishly. Ben caught his eye, nodded, and smiled. Seeing some form of validation, Donnie grinned and resumed watching the television, too.

As they followed the action on the screen, Mike faintly heard the doorbell ring and his mother greeting someone at the back entrance. His attention drifted back to the screen, and he let go with a *"Yaaaa!"* as a Rochester Nighthawk player scored a great behind-the-back goal. It took a few seconds, but he finally realized the rest of the room had grown quiet. When Mike turned away from the television, his smile faded. Standing in the doorway to the kitchen were his mother and Gwen Thrasher.

"Well, aren't you boys lucky," Jeannie said cheerfully. "This beautiful young lady says she's come to watch the lacrosse DVDs, too."

Mike didn't know who blushed the most, though he did see Gwen's face redden. His own face was hot, so he figured it was beet-red. When Mike turned away, he caught sight of Donnie, whose cheeks were a deep reddish-brown, while his eyes were the size of hubcaps. Later Donnie told Mike he was feeling "sympathetic embarrassment."

Gently, Jeannie pushed Gwen into the room. "Well, Gwen, I see some room by Mike over at the TV, so make yourself at home. I'll get you a glass of Coke and bring in some more chips."

Gwen nodded numbly and made her way over to where Mike sat. They glanced at each other shyly, then trained their eyes on the television.

The entire roomful of boys seemed stunned into silence at the sight of Mike and Gwen sitting together, then David shouted from the other side of the room, "Holy crap! Donnie farted!"

"Awwwwwwwwww!" everyone moaned, holding their noses and pushing Donnie.

"I did not!" Donnie cried, giving David a shove.

"Jeez, that coach looks like a walrus," Tommy said. "He's in half of the stuff on this DVD. His moustache is one big boogie catcher."

"That's Todd Lorenz," Mike said. "He lives in St. Albert and used to coach me. Spencer, his son, was on my team. Todd was an amazing player. He's in the Canadian Lacrosse Hall of Fame, and now he's one of the Edmonton Rush coaches."

All of the boys turned to Ben, who nodded in affirmation. They looked back at Mike with a new level of respect in their eyes.

"As a matter of fact," Donnie said, "Todd Lorenz won nine Senior A Mann Cups in thirteen years with the New Westminster Salmonbellies. When he played Intermediate A, he was the first player in Richmond, British Columbia, lacrosse history to score more than fifty goals in one season. He accumulated 857 points with the Salmonbellies. That's 380 goals and 477 assists."

"My God, Donnie!" Gwen cried. "Where do you come up with all of this stuff?"

"It's not stuff. It's important trivia. Mike mentioned Todd when we were shooting the ball around one day, so I Googled him."

Everyone once again turned and stared at Ben. Smiling, he shrugged and held up his hands. "The boy knows more than I do, but I think his numbers are right."

After that each time Todd Lorenz appeared on the screen everyone attempted to be the first to shout "Walrus!" as loudly as possible.

"Oh, man, watch this," Mike said. "This guy is Jimmy Quinlan from the Edmonton Rush." As Mike spoke, a player wearing a white-and-black jersey with number 81 across the back took the ball beside the net. Faking one way, he spun the other and drove hard to the net. When he reached the crease, he launched himself into the air and dived across in front of the net, flying horizontally while shooting the ball into the bottom corner for a goal.

"Ohhhhhhhh!" everyone gasped.

"You see, guys," Ben said, "you can't step into the crease, the circled area around the net, while you have the ball. What he did there was fly through the air above the crease and score before he hit the floor. If any part of him had touched the floor in the crease before the ball was in the net, it would be no goal."

"Man, I want to do that," Tommy said.

The gang continued to watch the DVD as clip after clip of spectacular goals flew by, then David said, "Hey, guys, let's go over to the school before it gets too late."

Everyone shouted agreement, jumped to their feet, and pushed past Ben in a scramble to get out of the living room.

Mike stopped as he passed his parents. "Thanks, Mom, Dad. That was great. Dad, you should come and watch these guys practise Arctic Sports. It's amazing. And you should see how good they are at lacrosse already."

"If your mom doesn't mind supper being a bit late, I might just do that." Ben glanced at Jeannie.

She kissed her husband. "Have fun."

Victor watched from the police yard as body after body tumbled out of the Watsons' back door. When Ben and Mike emerged, he waved. Mike waved back and ran over to Victor. "Hey, Victor!"

Victor nodded and smiled.

"*Sawubona*, Victor!"

Victor's smile turned to puzzlement.

"It's hello in Zulu. Cool, eh?"

"Very cool, Mike."

Ben caught up to Mike. "Hey, Vic, the boys are heading over to the gym to practise Arctic Sports and fool around with the lacrosse ball. Want to join us?"

"You know, Ben," Victor said, "I think I'll do just that."

Soon after they all arrived at the school gym, Mike started practising the airplane. Tensing his body on the floor, he gave his handlers the go-ahead and they lifted him about a metre off the ground. Then the boys slowly moved Mike around the edge of the gym, with Mike visibly fighting the urge to collapse. On he went until he finally collapsed as they lowered him to the floor.

Mike ran over and joined Ben and Victor. "What do you think?"

"You're a good Inuvialuit," Victor said, laughing.

Ben chuckled. "It looked great, son."

"Oh, man, Dad, watch this!" Mike pointed excitedly. "Tommy's going to do a high kick."

They watched as Tommy walked under the small toy seal hanging from the metal pole. He stretched his hand above his head and touched the seal with his fingertips. It was a full arm's length above him. Without turning his back he slowly stepped away, stopping when he felt comfortable with the distance. Rocking back and forth, he began to jog. As he reached the area in front of the seal, he swung his arms and sprang into the air. His right foot shot above his head, and the tips of his toes brushed the seal. Deftly, he landed back on his right foot and hopped in place with his arms in the air until he regained his balance.

"Isn't that something, Dad?" Mike asked.

Ben shook his head. "I don't believe it. That was out of this world."

"Hey, let's play some three-on-three!" David shouted.

The group ran to the lacrosse net and passed out sticks to the first two teams of three that would play. Some of the passes were off and the shots often went wild, but for not having played long they all looked really good. Gwen, in particular, seldom missed a pass unless it was completely wild, and every pass she made was perfect, every catch effortless. When she shot at the net, it was fluid and obvious that she was picking her spots. She wasn't good for a girl. She was just plain good. It was like watching poetry.

The boys laughed their heads off as they tried the moves they had seen earlier on the DVDs at Mike's house. Every so often Mike glanced over at his father when one of his new friends made a good pass or shot. Ben always smiled and nodded. The boys soon tired, but they had one last scrimmage that saw Tommy and Mike zip the ball back and forth so quickly no one could stop them.

Running hard, Tommy cut behind the net. "Ball, ball!" he shouted as he came around the other side.

Mike ripped a hard pass, and as it hit the mesh in Tommy's stick, he left his feet. In full flight he sailed in front of the net horizontal to the floor and popped the ball into the mesh. Landing hard, he rolled onto his back and raised his arms in the air. "Jimmy Quinlan scores!" he shouted.

Mike turned excitedly to see Ben's reaction. "Where did my dad go?" he asked, running over to Victor.

Victor shook his head. "I don't know. After Tommy pretended he could fly, your dad mumbled something under his breath and almost ran out of here."

Mike glanced at the large door. What had gotten into his father?

CHAPTER 17

His parents' voices didn't sound mad. They were animated, excited. Mike dropped his coat onto the floor of the porch and kicked off his boots along with his socks. Muttering to himself, he pulled his socks out of his boots and slipped them back onto his feet. Then he stood for a moment and listened.

"Ben, I know this has you excited, but don't you think you're jumping the gun a little?"

"No, I don't, Jeannie. You didn't see what I saw. These kids are amazing athletes. I mean, they can kick these little fuzzy seal things hanging way above their heads. And you should've seen Mike do this thing called the airplane. And that girl … Gwen. Oh, my God! Does she have hands! They just learned the game, and that Tommy kid scored a diving goal. His body control is astonishing."

"I know it seems exciting, Ben, but was there a goalie in the net? Were there boards that made the ball bounce back faster than they could react? Was there body contact? I'm not trying to be discouraging, but a team made up of kids who just learned the game …?"

Mike stepped around the corner. "Not all of them just learned the game, Mom. They have me."

"Mike, I don't want you boys to be disappointed," Jeannie said. "You don't really even have enough players for a full team."

"Yes, we do! I bet the guys from basketball at school would learn just as fast as Tommy and the rest. There's Mitchell Firth, Tyler Snowshoe, Bobby Vittrekwa, and Billy Greenland for a start. They all do snowshoe races and Dene games and stuff. And I bet one of the goalies who plays hockey would love to do something now that the season's pretty much over."

Ben nodded with a big grin.

"But it's already April, you two," Jeannie said. "You'd only have a couple of months before the Baggataway."

Mike's head snapped around at these words from his mother. "You're talking about taking a team to the Baggataway in St. Albert?" he squeaked.

Ben nodded.

"We'd play against Spencer and Cayln and we'd get killed," Mike said.

"You see, Ben," Jeannie said, "the boy knows. You have to face facts. I know you miss the game, but you can't —"

"From what I saw today, they wouldn't get killed," Ben insisted. "And so what if they didn't do great this year?" He turned to his son. "Mike, do you remember when you first started to play? The St. Albert teams always got killed when they went to British Columbia."

Mike nodded solemnly.

"But look at our ... the St. Albert teams now. They win and are just as competitive as anyone else. We've got kids here with more pure athletic talent than most southern kids. What a great foundation to start a team and a new sport for Inuvik."

Jeannie didn't say anything this time. The three grew quiet, all wrestling with their own thoughts.

"Dad's right," Mike finally said. "These are a great bunch of guys, and I want to do it if they do. I never thought I'd ever say it, but let's kick some St. Albert butt!"

Ben stood and high-fived Mike across the table.

Jeannie sighed. "Why do I even bother?"

* * *

Mike spread the word at school about starting a lacrosse team. Anyone interested was to come to the gym after school when the guys usually practised Arctic Sports. How many people would show up was a total unknown.

Mike sat beside his father on the edge of the stage at one end of the gym. They had been there for fifteen minutes, but it felt like an hour. He absently picked at a crack in the floor covering, trying not to squirm.

Ben glanced at Mike. "You sure everyone knows this is today?"

"Dad, we've only been here fifteen minutes. The guys are going to show up. They already love the game, and I know they'll be here."

"Do you think anyone else will come to see what it's all about?"

"I talked to the guys at basketball today, and they seemed pretty pumped. Guys get busy, though, so you never know."

The large main gym doors groaned on their hinges, and they both looked up. Ben held his breath and slowly exhaled as Donnie rushed inside. He waved excitedly and marched over to the stage. "Hey, guys! Boy, am I glad I'm not late."

Ben smiled, trying not to look too disappointed. "Donnie, I have a form here that you'll need to fill out. Just information on your age, height, weight, medical stuff, and getting permission from your parents."

A frown creased Donnie's face. "Why do I need to fill out a silly form?" His eyes got larger behind his glasses. "You think I'm here to play lacrosse?" He looked back and forth between Mike and Ben. "I'd die! I'm here to fill the position of manager."

Ben shrugged and tried not to betray the relief he felt.

"Mike says you guys are planning on playing in a tournament in St. Albert," Donnie continued. "That's going to take some money. I've done some rough cal-culations, and I figure with sixteen players, coaches, travel, hotel, and meals we'll need roughly twenty thousand dollars. That means fundraising and corpo-rate sponsorship."

As he spoke, Donnie became more animated, and his eyes seemed to spill out from around his glasses and expand over his cheeks. Ben drew his lips tightly together, fighting with every fibre in his body not to laugh.

"You're also going to need someone to look after training schedules, practice times, and nutrition." Donnie raised his hands. "I know, I know. I don't really look like a guy who'd know a lot about nutrition. I'm big-boned, you know."

Ben grimaced, swallowing hard to maintain control.

"But I've been on the Net studying nutrition for athletes, content and timing of meals varying with the intensity of training and the variability of time between games in a tournament setting. We can provide our team with what I'd call an engineered advantage by building and maintaining their systems at peak performance throughout the entire process." Donnie finally stopped and grinned at his captive audience of two.

"Don't you just love the big guy, Dad?" Mike said.

Ben nodded. "Welcome to the team, Donnie." He extended his hand to the huge kid, who almost lunged to clutch Ben's hand in an overenthusiastic shake.

Donnie's jubilation was interrupted by a ruckus at the main entrance to the gym. Both doors flew open as Tommy, David, Mark, Dennis Selamio, and Gwen entered at the same time.

"Hey!" they all shouted at once.

"We're here to sign up," Mark said as they approached.

Tommy laughed. "But only if we get huge signing bonuses."

Mike held up his fist. "Oh, I'll give you a bonus, all right."

Ben handed out forms and pens. Five. With Mike, six. It was a start. Then there was another commotion at the gym doors and six more boys marched through, bellowing greetings to those already present.

"Hey, Bobby!" Mike cried.

Bobby Vittrekwa waved back. "Hey, Mike!"

"We've never seen this lacrosse stuff, but Tommy says it's pretty cool, so we're here to give it a shot."

"That's fantastic!" Mike said. "This is my dad. Dad, this is Bobby Vittrekwa, Mitchell Firth, Tyler Snowshoe, Billy Greenland, and ..." He recognized the other two boys but didn't know their names.

Bobby stepped forward. "This is Ricky Alexie. He's a great hockey player and wins snowshoe races all over the place. He's like the Energizer Bunny. He just keeps going and going and going. This other guy is Grant Bonnetplume. From what Tommy told me I figured you might need a goalie. He's likely the best guy in our league, so he should do a pretty good job in lacrosse."

Ben shook the boys' hands. "Glad you could all make it. There are forms here for you to sign and take to your parents. Once they sign them, you'll need to bring them back to me. When these other guys are finished with the pens, please fill one out."

CHAPTER 18

Mike and his friends had two practices over the next four days. The boys and Gwen didn't have equipment yet, so they dressed in shorts and T-shirts. Between Ben and Mike, they managed to scrounge up nine sticks. Some were old and in rough shape, but for the time being they would have to do. They outfitted Grant in his hockey goalie gear and a pair of the largest hockey shin pads they could buy at the Northern Store. In lacrosse goalies wore shin pads like those of skaters in hockey, but much larger. Grant also had to use a regular lacrosse stick instead of a goalie stick, which had a huge basket and a longer shaft.

Ben outlined a crease around the net with masking tape, which gave the players a feeling for how close they could get. Then he had them take turns with the sticks and ran them through a series of basic, high-tempo drills: shuttle passing, scooping loose balls, placing checks and picks, rudimentary shooting skills, one-on-one battles for loose balls, and one-on-ones with a single player defending the net while the other player attempted to score.

The drills gave the boys and Gwen a chance to learn the basics and also helped Ben gauge the skill level of each player he was working with. In the end, Ben came up with an initial assessment of his players, along with some descriptions to keep track of who his players were.

MIKE WATSON (Right): Only player with game experience. Strong in all aspects. Offensively strongest. However, depending on other players, he might have to take on a more defensive role. Strong, fast, extremely intelligent on the floor, great shot.

TOMMY ALEEKUK (Left): Incredibly athletic. Short for his age and thick like Mike. Short black brush cut, big smile, darkest complexion on team, Inuvialuit. Amazing jumping ability, acrobatic, and tries new stuff. Very quick. Has mastered basic skills and has quickly gained higher knowledge of the finer aspects of the game.

MITCHELL FIRTH (Right): Another great athlete, but only now learning the basics. Average height, Gwich'in, long black rock-star hair. Small scar on chin, lighter skin, slight in build. Shaky skills at this stage, but cool on the floor. Extremely hard to get the ball from. Suspect will be a strong playmaker. Can already see him thinking through the game.

TYLER SNOWSHOE (Left): One of three lefties on team. Medium build, medium black hair, goofy smile, always joking and a little disruptive. Gwich'in. Different coloured eyes! One brown, one blue. Athletic and very aggressive. No equipment yet but loves to hit and is relentless going after the ball. Suspect he'll be a loose-ball vacuum once he masters the game. Skills coming very quickly.

DAVID ELANIK (Right): Tallish player. Light brown hair, quiet guy, very Asian, piercing blue eyes, Inuvialuit. Solid for his height. Struggling with skills but athletic. Medium speed but a thinker. Could be a good shooter if mind for the game continues to develop. With practice might develop like Mitchell as far as ball control.

BOBBY VITTREKWA (Right): Very tall and thin and extremely smooth. Gwich'in. Deceptive speed. Blows

197

by guys when he looks as if he's jogging. Wins faceoffs easily. Has the knack and looks as if he could play point. Another boy with a mind for the game and the athletic ability to back it up.

GWEN THRASHER (Left): The most incredible hands and skill. Inuvialuit. Beautiful kid, but has a bad temper that will need to be kept in check. Already making behind-the-back passes without even thinking. Can switch hands and shoot right without looking awkward. Solid, but it remains to be seen how she'll handle body contact in a real game.

BILLY GREENLAND (Right): Another kid who likes contact even without equipment. Average height and build. Gwich'in. Apparently a good hockey player, but needs to think lacrosse. A bit stubborn but should adjust. Very much a team player, which makes up for other things he lacks. A deceptively hard shot.

MARK KIKOAK (Right): There's strong and then there's strong. This kid is strong! Inuvialuit, with light skin and lots of freckles. Average height but very thick build like Mike's. Impossible to move off the ball. Very, very athletic and fun to be around. Piercing black eyes.

DENNIS SELAMIO (Right): Very polite Inuvialuit boy. Average height and build. White spot in hair on back of his head. Beautiful passer. Not a very strong shot, but every pass is on target and crisp.

RICKY ALEXIE (Right): Thin boy of average height. Gwich'in. Incredible endurance. Very strong work ethic that pushes the rest of the team. Never slows down and seems to love the game. Apparently spends much of his spare time on the land with his uncle and wins every snowshoe or cross-country ski race he enters. A born penalty killer!

GRANT BONNETPLUME (Goalie): Gwich'in boy of average height and build. Good reflexes and skill for a hockey goalie. Still adjusting to lacrosse stance and mentality. Having a terrible time with bounce shots and will need to work on that. Should be fine, but will needs lots and lots of work. Great passer.

CHAPTER 19

Mike and Ben pushed through the RCMP office door and stepped into the cold evening air. Pausing for a moment, Ben placed his hands on his hips and arched his back, exhaling loudly. "That sure was a long day," he told his son. "Thanks for coming by. You know, I'm really getting the hang of things now, and all the extra paperwork doesn't seem so bad, after all. And that lacrosse team! I've never seen a bunch of kids learn the game so quickly." Glancing to his left, Ben saw his blue RCMP pickup. "How about we go for a spin, Mike? I always find it helps me unwind before heading home."

"Sure, Dad."

Unlocking the door, Ben hopped into the driver's seat, waited for Mike to climb into the passenger seat, then started the engine. He threw the truck into reverse, backed into the street, and headed toward Mackenzie Road. The light was green, so he turned left and drove down Mackenzie to the centre of town. The streets were pretty much deserted at this time of night on a weekday.

"You know, Mike, I've been thinking. Now that things are getting easier at work, I'm going to spend more time with you and Victor at his camp, especially since the weather's getting better every day. That snowmobiling we did out to Victor's camp was a real treat, and I hear the boating in the summer is incredible."

Mike grinned and nodded. They were gliding by the Northern Store, and Mike smiled to himself when he recalled his mother's first reaction when she discovered it was *the* store in Inuvik. Continuing on, they passed Ingamo Hall before turning right and driving toward the residential area. Suddenly, Ben hit the brakes and skidded to a stop.

"What's wrong, Dad?"

"I'm not sure, but I thought I saw a light moving in one of the windows at Ingamo Hall."

Turning left, Ben continued for a block before making another left and then another back onto Mackenzie Road. He came to a halt opposite the hall and stared at the building.

"I don't see anything, Dad."

"Hmm, neither do I. Maybe it was just the reflection from my lights when I drove past. Still, I think I'll take a walk around the outside of the building just to make sure. You stay here. And I mean that, Mike. Stay here."

Mike watched his father hop out of the pickup and quietly close the door until the handle clicked. Looking both ways, he walked across the street and up along the right side of the building. His curiosity getting the better of him, Mike got out of the pickup and followed his father, who continued around the back, then stopped at the rear door.

Ben pushed the door, and it moved inward slowly. His father edged cautiously through the doorway, and Mike followed suit when his father disappeared into the building. As he passed through the doorway, Mike didn't see any sign of forced entry, something he knew about from his father. But he did notice that someone had taped over the recess in the lock so that it wouldn't engage when it was closed. As Donnie would say, Mike could feel his Spidey sense tingling. Allowing his eyes to adjust to the light inside the building, Mike moved farther inside, following his father's footsteps.

As Mike quietly moved through the rooms, nothing seemed out of order to him. Nothing was broken or smashed. When his father stopped in the kitchen, Mike hesitated just outside. On the counter there were at least five empty chip bags and cans of pop. When his father opened the fridge and peered inside, Mike saw that it was pretty much empty. From the microwave the smell of fresh popcorn was obvious. What type of thief, though, stopped to pop a bag of popcorn?

Leaving the kitchen, Ben continued his exploration of the rooms. As his father came to one last door, he hesitated again. It was partly open, and Mike saw a dim light flicker beyond the entrance. A television was on! Pushing open the door, Ben turned on the light.

A boy who had been lying on the couch leaped to his feet, wide-eyed and glaring. His fists were clenched, and it was pretty clear by the kid's expression that he was ready to bolt.

"Hey, there," Ben said, "I'm Sergeant Ben Watson. Watching some TV? I saw a light through the window and thought I'd check it out. If you don't mind, I'm going to sit over here." He motioned to an easy chair by the wall. Walking over, he casually sat down and turned to the boy. "Look, son, I don't know why you're in here, but right now I just want to talk. Why don't you sit down and we can see how things go?"

Just then Mike stepped into the room. "His name's Joseph Kiktorak, Dad."

Ben and Joseph both spun in the direction of the new voice.

"Mike, didn't I tell you to stay in the pickup?" Ben asked, almost scowling.

"I know, Dad, but —"

"You know this kid?"

"Yes, he goes to my school."

During all this, Joseph didn't move. Mike noticed that his face remained tense but that his fingers relaxed as he unclenched his fists. They all stared at one another for several long moments. Then, slowly, Joseph resumed sitting on the couch.

"Pleased to meet you, Joseph," Ben said.

Joseph grunted.

Looking beyond the boy, Ben nodded at the television. "Jeez, that's quite the set. These big screens are amazing. You've got the Oilers game on. I forgot they played tonight. What's the score?"

Joseph rolled his eyes in the direction of the television but didn't turn away from Ben or Mike. "The Oilers are up 3–2," he muttered.

Ben smiled. "Against Calgary, too. Battle of Alberta, man. It doesn't get any better."

The boy gazed at Ben, then quickly averted his eyes.

"Look, son, you know this is a break and enter, even though you haven't really messed anything up in here. You can't just go into places, eat food, and watch TV. That's what you do at home."

"I live with my granny," Joseph said, "and she doesn't have a TV. I just wanted to watch the game and then I was going home. I can pay for the chips and stuff. I ... I fixed the door with tape this afternoon. Can I go home now?"

"Actually, you can't, son," Ben said, shaking his head. "First of all, there's only five minutes left in the game and there's no way I'm going to leave before it's finished."

"I'm all for that!" Mike said a little too enthusiastically.

"I'm sure you are, Mike, but you and I are going to have a talk later about following orders."

A confused expression spread across Joseph's big face. It was obvious he didn't know how to read this situation.

Ben turned his attention back to Joseph, his face more serious now. "Son, I can't just let this go, though. I have to take you home and talk to your granny. Then I have to decide how we're going to handle all of this. Now let's watch this game and hope the Oilers can hold on."

Joseph stared at his feet, seemingly not paying attention to the action on the screen. With a minute left in the game the Flames pulled their goalie for a sixth attacker. For a moment Joseph seemed to forget his situation, raised his head, and followed the play as the Oilers held on for the victory.

Ben sighed and slumped back in the chair. "Now that's what they call an old-fashioned barn burner. Do you play hockey, Joseph?"

The boy looked up with passion in his eyes. "I do!" Then he frowned and let his massive shoulders sag. "I did …"

Ben nodded thoughtfully. "Were you any good?"

"I'm really good!" the boy said proudly, passion returning to his eyes.

"If you don't mind me asking, why did you quit, son?"

Mike knew the answer but thought it better if Joseph told his own story.

Joseph glanced at Mike, then gazed out the window, his mind appearing to wander off. Ben and Mike sat patiently, not wanting to push the boy for an answer. There was no rush. After a while, Joseph turned back. His eyes were watery, and he seemed close to tears. Taking a deep breath, he asked, "You're the new cop, aren't you?"

Ben nodded. "That's right."

The boy shrugged. "I got caught smoking pot. You don't have to say it. I know it was stupid. There were scouts, you know? Hockey scouts. They said I had it all. Everything they were looking for. I'm big, I can hit, I can shoot, I'm fast, and for a guy my size I've got pretty good hands." As if trying to prove the point, he stretched out his fingers.

"It was dumb," he continued. "I started to feel pretty big. A big fish in a little pond, my granny says. Some of the guys gave me booze and pot and whatever I wanted just to hang out with me. Everybody wanted to be my friend. It felt good, you know? My dad left when I was pretty young. He's from Tuktoyaktuk. I was just a kid with no dad until I found hockey. Then I lost all of that, and my mom had to move to Cambridge Bay for a job within a couple of months. That's when I started to live with my granny. No dad, no mom, no hockey, and no friends.

"It sucks! People suck! People just like you if they want something. Well, screw them all!" He glowered. "I don't need any of them. The same guys who sucked up to me are scared of me now. And that's fine by me. I don't need anybody." Close to tears once more, the boy turned to the window.

Coughing slightly, Ben got to his feet. "That's pretty harsh, Joseph. I can't imagine how all of that must hurt. But some lessons in life have to hurt, or they really wouldn't be lessons, would they? I don't expect you to answer that. I don't really know what's happened to you in the past. And I just met you tonight and not really under the best circumstances, either, if you know what I mean."

Ben's grin was infectious and inspired a slight smile from Joseph.

"I barely know you, Joseph," Ben said, "but you seem like a nice guy. I think you've got a lot of frustration built up inside and no way to let it out. I'll make a deal with you. I know Victor Allen pretty well. You probably know that he's on the Community Justice Committee. They use alternative sentencing, kind of like circle sentencing in some aboriginal communities. Mike and I are going to take you home, but we're not going to bother your granny with this tonight. I'm not going to write up a report, either."

Joseph stared at the floor and mumbled, "Thanks."

"You're going to go to school tomorrow and not miss any time there from now on. If you've been skipping any classes, you won't be doing that anymore. Are we clear on that?"

Joseph nodded.

"Okay, then, when I let you know, you'll have to come here and meet with the Community Justice Committee. I'll do my best to work something out with Victor, but you'll likely have to do something to make up for breaking into the hall. Understand, son?"

Joseph nodded. "Thank you, Mr. ... uh, Sergeant Watson."

"You can call me Ben from now on, Joseph. By the way, how old are you?"

"Fourteen."

"Jeez, you're big for your age," Ben said. "Mike's fourteen, too, and you make him seem short."

"C'mon, Dad," Mike said, "he's not that big!"

When Joseph got to his feet, he towered over Mike, causing everyone, including Mike, to chuckle. Ben then led the boys through the building to the back door. Stepping out, Ben turned to Joseph. "Close the door, son. But do me a favour. Take the tape off before you do."

Shooting Ben a guilty look, Joseph picked off the tape and stuck it in his pocket before closing the door behind him.

CHAPTER 20

At the next meeting of the Community Justice Committee, Ben and Victor spoke on Joseph's behalf. Some of the members were hesitant to provide the big boy with a second chance, but in the end things worked out. Joseph stood quietly while they explained what he would have to do: three months aiding elders with chores, no missing school for any reason, spending time assisting Victor at his camp, and helping Ben with the lacrosse team. It was a lot to expect, but Joseph accepted the verdict politely. Ben explained to Joseph that the lacrosse team had one of its most important practices the next night and that he should arrive at the gym no later than 5:00 p.m. There would be lots to do.

The next evening Mike, Donnie, Tommy, Bobby, Gwen, and the rest of the boys marched down the hall toward the gym. Mike knew what was up, but his father had asked him to say nothing until Joseph actually showed up at the gym. Ben had told the players that practice wouldn't be until 6:00 p.m. and that under no circumstances were they to get there any sooner.

Donnie, anxious as usual, was slightly ahead. Pushing one of the gym doors open, he stopped in his tracks, tugged the door shut again, and turned to face his friends. Mike had seen his eyes when he was excited and knew how big they could get. This time they were literally popping out of his head. His mouth hung open, and he kept mouthing something silently over and over again.

"What?" half of the players cried at the same time.

All Donnie did was motion over his shoulder and sputter.

Mike had a pretty good idea what had shocked Donnie, but he played dumb, anyway. "Jeez, Donnie, for Pete's sake, either spit it out or let us get by and see for ourselves. What's in there?"

Donnie gulped. "The ... the ... it's the Walrus!"

Now Mike really was stunned. He hadn't expected this. "Are you telling us Todd Lorenz is in there?"

Donnie nodded, but when Mike tried to push past he stopped him. "There's more!"

"What do you mean more?" Tommy demanded.

"Jimmy Quinlan's in there, too!"

"What?" everyone shouted in unison.

As they all shoved against Donnie, he held up his hands. "There's more!"

Everyone took a step backward and stared at Donnie.

"Jeez, Donnie, what more could there possibly be?" Bobby asked.

"They have piles of equipment and some kind of boards up at the end, and …" Sensing he was about to be crushed in a stampede, Donnie held up his hands once more. "And Joseph Kiktorak!"

Before anyone else could say anything, Gwen rammed through the crowd of boys to the front. "You're telling us the Walrus, Jimmy Quinlan, a pile of equipment, some type of lacrosse boards, and Joseph Kiktorak are all in the gym? Right here? Right now?"

Placing his hands on his hips, Donnie nodded, obviously pleased with himself.

"This I gotta see!" David Elanik cried, and the mob pushed past and through the doors behind him.

The scene at the far end of the gym was almost too much to fathom. Sure enough, there were temporary boards curved around the end of the gym and halfway up the sides. Todd Lorenz and Jimmy Quinlan were talking to Ben, and Joseph was carefully laying out piles of equipment and sticks. At the sound of the clattering at the gym doors the three men and Joseph glanced up.

Spotting Mike, Todd grinned. "Hey, Mr. Thick, you haven't grown a centimetre."

"Todd!" Mike shouted, running to shake his hand.

The rest of the gang followed and gathered around where the men and Joseph were standing.

"Guys … and Gwen," Ben said, "I'd like you to meet Todd Lorenz and Jimmy Quinlan. The Edmonton Rush, along with the National Lacrosse League, were nice enough to sponsor all of this equipment." He motioned to the piles scattered around them. "Todd and Jimmy were also nice enough to bring this stuff up here so they could put a clinic on for you guys at the same time."

"Mr. Lorenz, it's so unreal to meet you," Donnie gushed as he stepped forward. "I've studied all of your statistics. It's my belief that winning all those championships as a player-coach is one of the greatest sporting achievements on record."

"*Mr. Lorenz?*" Todd said, raising an eyebrow "I thought I was the Walrus."

Donnie's eyes practically left his head, and Todd laughed. In a few moments he was joined by everyone else in the hilarity.

"I hear some of you guys are pretty hot lacrosse players," Jimmy Quinlan said.

"In fact, I hear a guy named Tommy's trying to steal my job with the Rush."

Tommy blushed when everyone looked in his direction.

"I'm going to keep an eye on you, man," Jimmy added, pointing his stick at Tommy.

"Guys, we have to thank Victor Allen and a lot of volunteers who helped put these temporary boards together for us," Ben said. "Principal Dodson has agreed that we can keep these boards up until we leave for the Baggataway in June. That's just over a month, so we better thank him every chance we get. The boards have enough support and backing to give us some decent bounces and a feel for what it's like to get hammered a bit. There's going to be a lot of contact in this tournament, so we have to get used to it right away." Ben glanced at Joseph. "Joseph here is going to help us over the next few weeks as we get ready for the tournament. He's been nice enough to volunteer to help with water and equipment and all that stuff."

The group grew quiet as they watched Joseph neatly place one last pile of equipment. Straightening to his full height, he scowled at the boys. Then, with a trace of a smile, he waved before silently going back to his work.

"I've never seen the Monster smile before," Donnie whispered to Mike, who quickly elbowed him in the ribs and shot him an exasperated look.

"Okay, boys," Ben said, "let's get our equipment on and get busy. If you need help figuring anything out, ask Mike, Todd, Jimmy, or myself."

With a babble of excitement the boys hustled over to clumps of equipment and started the mystifying task of putting the stuff on for the first time in their lives. Todd, Jimmy, and Ben chuckled as the boys made some pretty big mistakes pulling on the kidney pads and other protection. Ben spied Joseph sitting near the stage, watching the other boys. He seemed a bit lost and not certain what to do.

"Hey, Joseph!" Ben called.

The big boy looked up.

"Why don't you put on the gear and give it a try?"

Joseph shook his head.

"Well, if you change your mind, you're welcome to join in," Ben said.

Once the boys had everything on in the right places, Todd and Jimmy went to work.

"Okay, gentlemen, let's see what you've got. Ben, get them to run some of the drills you've been working on so Jimmy and I can see what we're working with."

Ben had the boys do shuttle passes, breakouts, shooting drills, and loose-ball battles. With the equipment on, the intensity and contact picked up immediately. Jimmy and Todd stood back with Ben and watched.

Jimmy shook his head. "These kids are way ahead of where I thought they'd be."

Ben nodded. "Most of them are pretty gifted athletes. They do events called Arctic Sports that you wouldn't believe. That kid Tommy —" Ben motioned in Tommy's direction "— can jump in the air and kick a little stuffed seal way above his head and then land back on the foot he kicked it with. Mark over there is one of the strongest kids I've ever seen."

"You can see it when he gets in the corner after the ball," Todd said.

Jimmy nodded at the net. "My God, Ben! That girl ... Gwen, is it? She has the most amazing hands. Watch this, watch this!"

As Jimmy spoke, Gwen calmly scooped up the ball and faked Mike out of his shoes. Cutting across in front of Grant in the net, she flipped a pass back over her shoulder that hit dead centre in the mesh of Mitchell's stick. It surprised him, and after a quick glance into his basket, he easily plopped the ball into the open side of the net.

"*Whoooooo!* Way to go!" Todd yelled, holding his arms above his head. "Okay, folks, let's start some serious hitting."

The next part of the practice was fast and furious. Once the players got rid of the urge to lunge at each other and flail all over the place, they learned quickly how to administer solid body contact, and the three coaches stood back in amazement.

"These kids are truly amazing," Jimmy said. "They learn so fast it's unreal."

David Elanik, who was jogging by, suddenly stopped. "My dad says that aboriginal people learn best by watching. For years before we went to schools and stuff, we depended on being observers of the land, animals, and our elders. To this day you show us how to do something and we'll learn it right away." He shrugged and joined the other players in line beside the net.

Todd was a fantastic teacher, and the players loved him. He had an easy, likable manner that endeared him to the kids in minutes. Jimmy was much the same way and made the players feel comfortable and eager to learn. As the practice wound down, Ben called everybody to the centre of the gym and had them kneel around Todd and Jimmy.

While Jimmy went over some last-minute advice on the two pick plays they had shown the players, Todd nudged Ben with his elbow and nodded over the players' heads at the net. Ben followed Todd's gaze and spotted Joseph holding one of the lacrosse sticks gently in his hands. He turned it over and over, running his hand along the shaft. Walking slowly, he approached one of the balls lying on the floor and deftly scooped it up. Rotating his wrists, he moved the basket back and forth, cradling the ball as he strode away from the net. Halting, he turned and stared at the net. Quickly moving the stick up and down, he flipped the ball into the air and caught it a few times.

By now the players had caught on and were watching Joseph, too, as he continued to juggle the ball. Suddenly, he reared back and fired the ball at the net. Like a laser beam, it ripped with incredible velocity into the top corner of the net, bulging the twine and making a *fwooosh!* sound that echoed throughout the gym.

"Whooooooo!" Todd shouted as the players gasped.

"Holy crap!" Jimmy said. "You guys are trying to beat me out of a job. That was harder than any shot I've ever made."

Joseph looked at all the awed faces. "If it's okay, I'd like to join the team." He turned the lacrosse stick in his hands. "This feels right."

CHAPTER 21

After the visit from Todd and Jimmy, the team grew even closer. The players went to school together, practised together, and hung out together. Everyone got along, something that would be very important when they travelled south.

The tournament was only a few weeks away. The weather and daylight had made a dramatic shift from March when the Watsons first arrived. The temperature was above or close to zero every day now. In March they had at best experienced nine to ten hours of sunlight. Now there was more than eighteen. By June they would have twenty-four hours.

Donnie, in his usual wide-eyed fashion, informed Mike that in January when Inuvik experienced zero hours of daylight, New York had just over nine hours. In March when Inuvik had almost ten hours of daylight, New York had eleven. But in June when Inuvik had twenty-four hours of daylight, New York only had a bit under fifteen. He claimed that if you added it all up, Inuvik was a much sunnier place. Mike had learned not to doubt things said by Donnie and could only nod with interest when he told him all this stuff.

And the light was intense! It shone brightly every morning, and the town's spirits seemed to lift higher with the increasing warmth. Each day the snow shrank and the river ice began to break up. Apparently, it had already broken at Tsiigehtchic, and Inuvik's time couldn't be far off. Victor had promised that before the team left for the tournament he would take the players by boat to his camp for a send-off celebration.

Mike revelled in the competition and camaraderie as he went up against Joseph or Gwen in practice. They would hammer at one another and have the most extreme confrontations, but it would always end in laughter and a lot of good-natured fooling around on the floor. Donnie's eyes almost crossed one day, too, when he walked past Joseph and the huge kid reached out and playfully messed his hair. The Monster had been tamed!

What at first seemed like a major disaster, however, took place at one of the team's last practices before they were scheduled to leave town. Grant had been growing in confidence between the pipes but hadn't adjusted as quickly to lacrosse as Ben had hoped. He was getting better but was still the one weak spot on the team. A good goalie made a huge difference in lacrosse, and not having Grant adapt to the position hurt the team's chances of having a decent showing at the tournament.

Each practice session had several shootouts as a fun break from the more intense drills. The shootout continued until only one player was left. Tommy, Gwen, Joseph, and Mike were the last ones on this particular occasion. Mike rushed in first and tried a fancy bounce shot between his legs that failed miserably. Gwen went next. Crossing in front of the net, she faked a shot before deftly whipping the ball back over her shoulder, rippling the mesh behind Grant. The rest of the team cheered wildly. Joseph jogged toward the net, then unexpectedly reared back and rifled a long-distance shot as hard as he could. It caught Grant by surprise, and for some reason, despite all of the practice, he tried to catch the ball with his free hand hockey style. Big mistake! Lacrosse goalies didn't have a catching mitt like those of hockey goalies. They had two gloves pretty much the same as players who ran the floor, and there wasn't much padding in the palm.

Grant's cry of pain echoed off the gym walls as he threw his gloves into the air and fell to his knees, holding his injured hand close to his chest. Ben and Victor, who had been watching the practice, raced over and knelt beside Grant, examining his hand as the team crowded around.

Ben turned ashen-faced to Victor and whispered, "Vic, I think he has at least two broken fingers."

"You stay with the boys, Ben," Victor said. "Let me take him to the hospital. You finish what you started here while I take care of the boy."

Ben nodded and got to his feet. "Boys, stand back and give Mr. Allen and Grant room. We're going to get Grant to the hospital to get him checked out, but the rest of you need to finish practice."

The team solemnly stepped back as Victor helped Grant out of his equipment and hurried him off to the hospital. Everyone stood in a daze for a few moments, not really quite sure what to do.

"Dad, what are we going to do for the rest of the practice?" Mike asked. "Today you said we were going to pretty much concentrate on shooting. Now we don't have a goalie. Jeez, if Grant's hurt bad we might not even have a goalie for the tournament."

Ben held up his hand for Mike and the rest of the players to listen. "Let's not get carried away until we know for sure how hurt Grant is. For the moment what we need is somebody to stand in for Grant."

Ben looked at his players, and they returned his stare. Gwen elbowed Mike, and he nodded, then glanced at the stage. Soon everybody's attention, including Ben's, was focused where Donnie sat mulling over shooting percentages and other statistics.

Glancing up at the team when he noticed the sudden silence, Donnie realized the whole team was watching him. His cheeks flushing, he cried in exasperation, "I didn't fart!"

A few of the players snickered as Ben approached Donnie. "Nobody says you farted Donnie. You're an important part of this team. And being a member of the team, you can be called upon to do different things depending on the situation. As of this minute, we have a different situation. We need a warm body in the net."

"Oh, n-no, n-no!" Donnie stuttered. "I'm not a warm body. I'm not much of a body at all. I saw what happened to Grant, and I don't want to die." He pointed at the team. "I won't let them kill me!"

Ben placed a hand on Donnie's shoulder reassuringly, then looked at the rest of the team. "If Donnie goes in the net, anybody who hits him hard with the ball has to sit out for five minutes. In other words, he stands there with the equipment on and you guys pick the corners around him. He doesn't have to move and he doesn't have to be afraid of one of you smacking him with the ball. Got it?" Everyone nodded, and Ben turned back to Donnie. "See, big guy? Everybody's behind you on this. We need you for this one practice. Can you do it?"

Donnie blinked in blurry hugeness behind his glasses. "Yes," he said, sighing. "I don't believe I'm doing this, but yes!"

"Thataboy!" Ben said, clapping him on the back. "Okay, guys, let's get Donnie suited up."

Gwen and Mike led Donnie to the equipment and helped bundle him up. The equipment was a bit sweaty from Grant, and Donnie grimaced as the cold wetness of the recent sweat touched his skin. Clad in his new suit of armour, he waddled over to the net and turned around.

Tyler Snowshoe gasped. "Jeez, he's big in there!"

It was true! With Donnie's size there didn't seem to be a whole lot of net to shoot at.

"You okay, Donnie?" Ben asked.

"Yes, Mr. Watson," Donnie said without much enthusiasm.

"Mike," Ben said, "show Donnie how to stand."

224

"I know how to stand!" Donnie cried. "I watch Grant every day. I've seen the DVDs." As if to emphasize his point, Donnie placed the blade of the goalie stick on the floor and put his left hand on his hip. He actually looked like a lacrosse goalie!

"Okay, everybody," Ben said, "get into lines. Time for passing plays."

The players started to run some plays and were careful not to hurt Donnie. He took a few shots off the chest pad, and when he didn't feel any pain, decided to keep his eyes open. Ben smiled and walked over to the stage to write a few notes.

A few minutes later Mike tugged at Ben's sleeve. "Dad, get your head out of your papers and watch this!" He pointed to the action at the other end of the gym.

Ben turned in time to see Gwen, Joseph, and Tommy moving toward the net. Donnie stood in perfect lacrosse fashion and watched as the three players moved the ball around the crease. Joseph quickly passed the ball over to Gwen, and Donnie shifted to that side. Gwen immediately flipped the ball to Tommy, who one-timed a shot at the open net. In acrobatic fashion Donnie flopped back and snapped his goalie stick across, catching the shot in the huge pocket of mesh.

Ben gasped. "Holy crap! How long has he been doing that?"

"Since about the fourth shot!" Mike cried excitedly.

Ben strolled to the other end of the gym as each line ran in on Donnie, trying to score. Mike faked a pass to Mark and fired a bounce shot to Donnie's left. The big boy flicked his leg out and took the ball off the toe of his shoe. Gwen, Mitchell, and Billy worked the ball around until Gwen caught a pass in full flight in front of the net, flipping a shot over her shoulder. Donnie threw his upper body in the way, and Gwen swung her stick in anger at the post.

"There's no place to shoot!" she cried in exasperation to Ben. "He covers the whole darn net!"

Mike laughed. "He's also covering the angles like a monster cat."

Ben blew his whistle and walked over to Donnie. All that could be seen of Donnie's face were eyes and cheeks pushing against the inside of his mask. "Who the heck are you and what have you done with Donnie?" Ben mock-demanded. "You're amazing!"

Donnie tapped his stick nervously on the floor. "I don't really know, but ... but I watched Grant a lot, you know? I watched this stuff on YouTube, too. I kind of ... I don't know ... I kind of pretended at home I was Steve "Chugger" Dietrich, the NLL goalie. He's bigger like me, and he's a great goalie. I guess I day-dreamed a bit that maybe … I dunno … that maybe I could really be part of this team."

"Well, my friend, Mr. Donnie," Ben said, placing a hand on each of Donnie's massive shoulders, "if Grant isn't able to play, your daydreams may just come true."

Donnie's head snapped up, surprise and joy in his eyes simultaneously. "Are you serious?"

"Of course, he's serious," Tommy said over Ben's shoulder. "Now get back in net, because one way or another I'm finally going to score on you."

Donnie squinted at Tommy. "Let's see you try," he said as he lumbered back between the pipes.

CHAPTER 22

As it turned out, Grant's index finger and thumb were both broken, and he was done as a player. The boys were all pretty choked, but Donnie's first experience in the net hadn't been a fluke. At every practice he grew in confidence and became harder and harder to score on. He was big and played the angles flawlessly. It made him an imposing figure in the net. And in true Donnie style he studied everything he could put his hands on: YouTube videos, the DVDs Mike had at home, and anything else he could find on the Internet. Mike told Ben that at recess one day in the boys' bathroom Donnie was standing on a toilet with the stall door propped open so he could see his full body in the mirror. He was in his goalie stance, shifting back and forth. When Mike burst in, Donnie stumbled off and clattered to the floor.

There were a few things Donnie had to work on, like stepping out of the net to meet long shots and moving back against the crossbar when players had the ball in close, but he was indeed very good. With the exception of Mike, though, Donnie lacked what all the other players were short on — experience in a real game. How would they react against another, more experienced team? Would they be intimidated? They looked great in practice, but once an actual game came along would they disappear into the woodwork?

The ice on the Mackenzie River had finally broken up, and Victor invited everyone to his camp for a team getaway before they left for Edmonton and St. Albert. There was now more than twenty hours of daylight, and the weather was fantastic. It took three boats, but Victor, Ben, and the team finally arrived at Victor's camp for a one-night getaway. It was a great team-building experience, and Mike was thrilled to see the terrific camaraderie among his fellow players.

Ben had purchased a second-hand boat from another RCMP officer who had transferred south, and this trip was his first chance to try it out. Mike was ecstatic when Ben turned the wheel over to him for part of the trip. Nothing could wipe the smile off Mike's face. When they reached Victor's camp, Joseph was on the shore to greet them and help land the boats. He had been helping Victor and several other elders over the past few weeks and actually seemed to enjoy the work.

It was late in the day, and Joseph had a fire going on the shore. Mike and Ben smelled fish cooking as they ambled up from the boats. The team settled around the fire as Victor and Joseph prepared a meal and refreshments. Mike gazed across the river, then looked around the fire at the happy faces of his teammates. "This is all pretty sweet," he whispered, leaning close to his father.

Ben smiled. "You're right, son. It's pretty nice, isn't it?"

"I'm sorry I was so ... I don't know ... crappy to you and Mom when we first moved here. I never guessed it would be like this. It really feels like home now."

Ben wrapped his arm around Mike's shoulders and pulled him close. "It does, doesn't it?"

Gwen grabbed a soft drink from the table near Victor's cabin and strolled back to the fire. Hesitating for only a moment, she plunked down beside Mike. He glanced over and smiled before turning back to

Tommy, who was sitting across and to the other side of Ben. Gwen took a sip and waited for the right moment. Even though they had gotten to know each other better, they really hadn't spoken much except to yell for passes or smack each other on the back when one of them scored a goal. But at least they were on friendly terms now. "Hey, Mike," she said.

"Hey, yourself, Gwen." The flames from the fire reflected in her eyes, and Mike felt his face flush. "This is great, isn't it? I love it every time I come out here with Victor."

Gwen nodded, then peered at the fire before turning to Mike. "I ... I'm sorry I treated you so badly when you first moved here. I shouldn't have. It's just ... well, things happened when I was young. I ..."

"You don't have to explain anything, Gwen. We all have things that bug us from time to time. I was pretty weird when we moved here, too. I hated this place and didn't even know what it was all about. I hated it because I had to leave all my ... my old friends in St. Albert. Pretty stupid when you think about it. This place is great, but I hated it, anyway."

"My dad was from the South," Gwen said. "He left when I was seven and never came back. He never wrote, never called. He doesn't even know what I look like now." Gwen's voice quavered as she looked away.

Slowly, she turned back to Mike. "If you had a daughter, wouldn't you want to know what she looked like?"

Mike nodded. "I sure would. Your dad doesn't know what he's missing. I mean ... you're great."

Gwen touched Mike's arm. "Mike, I've hated everybody who ever moved here from the South. I hated them all because they made me think of my father. That's why I hated you. But no matter what I did, you're the first person who didn't run away or avoid me. You kept being nice to me." She paused. "Thank you. You don't know how much it means." Gwen stood, then leaned close to Mike's ear. "And that kiss was really nice!" Spinning on her heel, she walked briskly around the fire toward the cabin.

Mike's face burned like wildfire. He suppressed a nervous giggle as he returned his attention to where Tommy and Donnie were sitting. The two boys were staring at Mike, and Tommy's eyes were almost as big as Donnie's. Donnie whispered something to Tommy and then they both pursed their lips and made smacking sounds. Mike shook his head and tried to look mad, but he started laughing, anyway.

Ben stood and moved to the edge of the fire. Holding up his hands for quiet, he said, "First of all, I'd like to thank Victor ... and Joseph for making it so nice out here for us tonight. The food's great, the company's fantastic, and this —" he indicated the sky and the river "— is unbelievable. A few months back I don't think Mike or I imagined we'd be somewhere as beautiful as this." He pulled a piece of paper out of his pocket. "This is our schedule for the tournament, and it isn't easy. Our first game is against St. Albert."

There was a slight sigh from the group and then everyone looked at Mike.

He shrugged and smiled. "Hey, man, if we're going to kick some St. Albert butt, it might as well be in the first game we play."

"Yay!" Donnie yelled a little too enthusiastically. Tommy bumped him with his shoulder, but everyone nodded around the fire.

"Our next three games are against Leduc, the Edmonton Warriors, and then Red Deer," Ben said. "All good teams. But from what I've seen, we can beat everyone if we execute what we've learned and play like a team. Lacrosse is a game of control and a game you win as a team. If we win most of the loose-ball battles, play good D, and control the ball, we're going to be tough in every single game."

Walking to the edge of the circle of players, Ben bent over and clutched a balled-up piece of clothing to his chest as he headed back to the fire. "I wanted this to be a surprise. Donnie came up with the name.

Someone told me that Gwen was quite the artist, so I asked her to keep it a secret and had her draw up the logo. Victor was good enough to get a couple of local businesses to sponsor the cost of having them made. Guys, I'd like to introduce you to your team jersey!" He held the jersey high and let it fall out to full form.

There were a few "Whoas!" and "All rights!" around the fire as the players talked excitedly among themselves. The jersey was black and gold like the Boston Bruins' hockey jersey. The logo was a player in a parka holding a lacrosse stick as if he were about to throw a cross-check. The expression on the face was an aggressive snarl. Above the logo was INUVIK and below that was ARCTIC THUNDER.

"Now for the cool part," Ben continued. "Remember when you guys told me what numbers you wanted a while back? Well, look at this." He turned the jersey around. In the middle there was a big number 33. Across the shoulders was DEBASTIEN.

Ben laughed. "Officially, welcome to the team, big buddy." He held the jersey out to Donnie.

For once Donnie's eyes weren't enormous. In fact, they were closed. A single tear squeezed out of the corner of his left eye and trickled down his cheek. Blindly, he held out his hand into which Ben placed the jersey. He hugged it to his chest.

Tommy patted Donnie on the back. "Congratulations, Donnie. You're an amazing goalie and just about one of the nicest guys I know. I'm sorry it took me so long to see that. I wouldn't want to be on a team without you."

The rest of the players nodded.

"Yay, Donnie!" Tyler cried.

"You da man, Donnie!" Bobby added.

Ben then presented each player with a jersey. When the jerseys were all distributed, the kids gazed at them proudly. Then Joseph got to his feet, cleared his throat, and said, "Guys, I guess I've been a bit of a creep to all of you."

Mike nodded in exaggerated fashion.

Joseph glared at him. "You don't have to agree that much! But, Sergeant Watson, I mean, Coach, I want to thank you for giving me a chance on this team. And, Mike, thanks for bringing lacrosse with you to Inuvik. Most of us didn't know anything about what a great game it is. Most of us didn't have any idea what a great guy Donnie was before you got here. I was mad at the world because of problems I made for myself, and … well …" He smiled mischievously. "Well, nobody knew Gwen had a heart, Mike, until you kissed her!"

The boys all laughed. Gwen shook her fist at Joseph. It was hard to tell who was blushing the most

— Mike or Gwen. Joseph turned red, too, but mostly from laughing at his own joke.

"Thanks, Coach," Joseph continued, "and thanks, Victor, for believing in me when no one else did. I won't let any of you down. I won't repeat the mistakes I've made. I promise. I have to admit I'm pretty confused. I don't really know what I'm going to do in the future, and sometimes ... I don't know ... I don't even know what it feels like to be Inuvialuit or anything. I mean, I've been so busy thinking first about making the NHL and then feeling sorry for myself that I don't even remember how to speak my own language anymore. I guess I'm still a bit lost, but I have this feeling that things are going to get better."

"How do you know where you're going if you don't know where you've come from?" Everyone turned as Mike stood. Gulping, he said, "You know, if it hadn't been for Victor and Donnie and my dad, none of this would be happening. Victor said that to me, you know, about knowing where I came from, and it really got me thinking about life and what was important and everything else. Before that I was being a bit of a jerk, too, hating Inuvik and only thinking of myself and my ... well, the friends I used to have in St. Albert. I started to think about what makes me, well, me.

"Some of my heritage is Zulu. Did you guys know there was a Zulu chief many years ago named Shaka? He was the first great Zulu chief. The reason he was great was because he pulled all the Zulu people together as one. And as one, nobody could beat them. They had just been all these individual tribes before — individual with no power." He stopped and saw Victor and Ben exchange glances.

"Shaka was fearless, and by making all the tribes see they were more powerful working together, the Zulu became the most fearsome group in all of South Africa. Together they came up with new battle strategies and all kinds of stuff to beat their enemies. We're all kind of like that. Some of us were mad before. Some of us didn't understand each other. Now we're a team and we see how great we all are. If we play together the way we're all getting along here tonight, nobody, not even St. Albert, is going to beat us."

Bobby stood and looked directly at Ben. "Coach, I know we haven't really talked about this yet, but I think it's time. I think …" He glanced at Mike, then back at Ben. "I vote that 'Shaka' be the captain of Arctic Thunder."

Donnie jumped to his feet. "So do I!"

Tommy stood along with Gwen. "So do I!" they said together.

One by one the players rose to their feet and repeated, "So do I!"

"Well, everyone, it's settled," Ben said. "Mike … Shaka, congratulations. You're the first captain of Arctic Thunder."

"Ya!" everyone cried.

Mike shuffled his feet, trying hard not to show how pleased he was.

As everyone settled back around the fire, Victor rose to his feet. Everyone grew silent. "This all makes me very proud. Arctic Thunder is a strong team in body and in spirit. Gwich'in, Inuvialuit, Zulu, and others are all gathered together. Different cultures but strong cultures, ones that know the land and have relied on their ties to it to survive. The Inuvialuit came from Alaska and survived thanks to the life given by the sea and the land. They relied on each other, with the women fishing, the men hunting, and families working together to survive. The Gwich'in are also people of the land. They, too, have endured hardships like harsh climate and horrible disease that reduced their numbers greatly. But the Inuvialuit and the Gwich'in are strong cultures. We're cultures of the North, and we survived. Our cultures have survived and our numbers have grown with our strength.

"The Zulu culture is a strong culture, too. It's also a culture that has lived with the land and undergone great hardships. And the Irish —" he smiled at Ben "— is another strong culture full of heritage and pride. Joseph, Mitchell, Donnie, Gwen, Mike, Mark, all of you, it's important that you know and understand your cultures. It's important that you can speak your language and practise your traditions. That's how you'll learn to understand yourself, and that's where you'll gain the strength that will go with you to St. Albert where I know you'll kick some butt!"

Mike studied the fire, lost in his own thoughts. He was going to play lacrosse again. This time against St. Albert!

CHAPTER 23

The plane trip south was a riot. Some of the boys had been on a big plane before and others hadn't. If anyone was nervous, it didn't show. Ben had his hands full, but thankfully there was help from a few parents who had agreed to come along for the tournament. Other than the odd peanut or cookie thrown at a teammate and the noise level that at times became unbearable for some of the other passengers, there were no major disasters.

When they arrived in Edmonton, two vans were waiting to take the players directly to their hotel in St. Albert. Ben had told Mike that he didn't want the team to face too many distractions before the upcoming tournament. They would have time to visit the

West Edmonton Mall and other sites before they flew home. As it was, their game against St. Albert was the next afternoon. The *St. Albert Gazette* and the *Edmonton Journal* had already contacted Ben to see if they could interview Arctic Thunder players. With reservations Ben had agreed but only after their first game with St. Albert was out of the way.

The noise level escalated as the vans drove through the city. When the boys spotted the West Edmonton Mall, they went berserk.

"Oh, man!" Tommy shouted from the back. "Donnie farted again!"

Ben turned to scold Tommy and try to settle things down.

"I actually did this time!" Donnie cried gleefully. "Taste the wrath of the Donster!" The windows of the van were quickly rolled down amid howls and groans. Ben actually stuck his head out the window at one point. The flight had been slightly turbulent, and the "Donster" was mighty ripe!

It was late afternoon by the time the team was checked in at the hotel. A quick supper was arranged at Boston Pizza, and Ben made sure the team was quickly settled in for the night. No one complained. They were excited but apprehensive about the next day. It was well after midnight before Mike finally fell asleep.

The team had a late breakfast the next morning and then bussed to the Servus Place Sports Complex, which had three ice surfaces, two indoor soccer fields, a running track that went around the top of the building, an exercise and weight area, and a pool with water slides. When the boys stepped into the main arena where the opening ceremonies and their first game would take place, their mouths dropped open. They looked down on rows of red high-backed seats encircling the playing surface. Mike told them the arena could hold twenty-five hundred people, not including standing room.

David gasped. "This is unbelievable! More than half the population of Inuvik could sit here and watch us play."

"And it's going to be pretty full for the first game against St. Albert," Ben said. "The home team against a team from the Northwest Territories in the opener will be a big draw. It's going to be a bit distracting, guys, but we have to get over that and concentrate on the game."

Joseph wandered over and stood beside Mike. "This is where St. Albert's Junior A hockey team plays, isn't it?" It was more of a comment than a question.

"That's right, Joseph," Mike said.

"Man, I blew it!" Joseph shook his head as he took in the seats and huge clock hanging over the playing surface. He turned to Mike. "You know what, though? I think this means more to me than anything else could. I won't let you down, Mike. I have a lot to make up for, and it's going to start here. Maybe I'll get another chance at hockey and maybe I won't, but I love this." He held up the lacrosse stick he was carrying. "For some reason this feels right."

Mike nodded. "I feel the same way, Joseph. Once you get lacrosse under your skin, it's hard to shake. Wait until you get your first big hit this afternoon. Wait until you score your first goal. It only gets better."

The boys didn't have much time to talk. They were soon hustled under the seats to a dressing room where they stored their equipment. After a short wait, the festivities began.

The opening ceremonies were a blur. The teams were led in by people carrying their club names on banners. When the Arctic Thunder players were announced, they marched onto the floor and received the loudest ovation next to the one St. Albert got.

It was all very emotional for Mike. The guys from St. Albert spotted him and waved. Spencer, Cayln, Taylor, Ryan, and the rest of the guys came over and shook Mike's hand. It was a bit awkward, too. Mike was incredibly happy to see his old buddies, but he didn't want it to appear that he was favouring them over his new teammates. He felt a little stiff standing there and was relieved when the guys had to go back to their spot for the national anthem and a speech from the mayor of St. Albert. It all ended quickly and then it was time to get dressed for the game.

The team elected Tommy and Bobby to be assistant captains, and with ten minutes left before faceoff, Ben voiced his final comments. "Okay, guys, listen up! This is your first game. Things are going to seem a lot faster than in practice. Just stay calm and keep your heads in the game and you'll be fine." He paced across the room, then turned to the players. "When they have the ball, we run back and box it up. When there's a loose ball, it's ours. We win it." A buzzer sounded outside the dressing room. "That's it, guys! Time to get on the floor. And remember, this isn't a practice against your buddies anymore. The hitting is for real. So keep your heads up and don't be afraid to hammer somebody out there. Let's go!"

"Let's go, man!" Mike shouted.

"Let's go, Inuvik!" Tommy yelled.

As they ran through the tunnel and out under the harsh lighting on the floor, some of the boys couldn't help but stop and stare. The seats were almost full, and it seemed as if they were surrounded by a sea of faces.

"Get moving, Donnie!" Mike yelled at the big boy as he jogged past. "Snap out of it. You gotta get warmed up!"

The warm-up went quickly. The mayor returned to the floor, and the captains were called to centre for an official faceoff. Mike met Spencer with the referee, and they shook hands awkwardly.

"This seems pretty weird," Spencer mumbled under his breath.

"I know," Mike said, "but I'm gonna knock you on your butt!"

Spencer grinned as the boys bent for the faceoff. Spencer being captain for the home team drew the ball back before picking it up and handing it to the mayor. Mike and Spencer shook hands again and wished each other good luck before jogging back and rejoining their respective teams. It was game time!

Ben started Mike with Mitchell and Tyler, along with Joseph and Mark as shooters. Kneeling for the faceoff, Mike glanced up to see Ryan Domino smirking at him from the other side of the ball. "Ready to lose, Mike?"

"I was going to ask you the same thing, Domino." Despite his smile, Mike felt a cold, queasy tempest in his stomach.

The referee backed away and blew his whistle. Ryan dug in and pulled the ball behind him where

Cayln was waiting. Mitchell seemed to freeze, and Cayln darted past, throwing a quick pass up to Taylor.

"Box it up!" Ben shouted.

Taylor whipped the ball across to Spencer, who threw a pass over to Scott. Shifting his weight forward, Scott stepped into a shot that rippled the net before Donnie even moved. The fans and the Rams' bench erupted in cheering.

"Time, Ref!" Mike yelled at the referee. "Time out!"

Blowing his whistle, the referee pointed at the Inuvik bench to signal who had called a timeout.

"Run it in!" Ben cried. "Run it in!"

Mike led the way, and they huddled around the front of the bench.

"Okay, everybody," Ben said, "that was your one wonderstruck goal. You're over it. Now let's get our heads into the game and settle down. Beat them to the ball. Let's go, Thunder!"

The boys all stuck their gloves into a circle and cried, "One, two, three, Thunder!"

"Let's change things up," Ben said. "I want Tommy, Gwen, and Bobby, with Joseph and Ricky as shooters. Hustle out!"

Tommy lined up across from Taylor to kneel for the faceoff. When the referee blew his whistle, Tommy pushed Taylor away from the ball. Blowing his whistle again, the referee signalled that it was the Rams' ball. Tommy straightened, puzzlement in his face as he jogged back to his own net.

Taylor scooped up the ball and raced into the Inuvik end. With a burst of speed he slipped into the corner, spun, and passed the ball to Spencer, the shooter. Spencer faked a shot and moved the ball across to Scott. Arctic Thunder had a box set up and were doing a good job of keeping the Rams outside. All at once Brady and Cayln crossed in front of the net, switching sides. Cayln posted up and spun for a pass. Brady, who was incredibly fast, jogged behind the net and out the other side. The manoeuvre confused the Thunder, and no one stuck with Brady. The pass from Scott hit Brady's stick flush in the basket, and he quick-sticked the ball at the top corner. Donnie reacted rapidly, flicking his big stick across, but he only partially blocked the shot. It tipped off the end of his stick and into the net. The Rams were up 2–0, with only two minutes off the game clock.

"You've got to switch, guys," Ben said to the players as they came to the bench to change up. "You've got to switch and talk to each other out there." There was a bit of chaos, and the Thunder only sent four players out for the next faceoff.

"Not enough guys, Dad," Mike said, heading for the gate.

Ben grabbed Mike by the jersey. "Hang on a second, son. Let's see if Dennis can win the draw."

Backing up, the referee blew his whistle. Dennis dug down and leveraged the ball toward his own net so that Mark could scoop it up.

"Break, Mike, break!" Ben said, pushing Mike out of the box. Mike sprinted as fast as he could toward the Rams' net.

"Ball, ball!" he cried, looking over his shoulder. Dennis spotted Mike and launched a long-range pass as hard as he could down the floor. Glancing over his shoulder, Mike accelerated, judging that he would have to run at top speed to receive the pass. He was right, and his timing was perfect. His heart leaped into his chest as he realized he was going to catch the pass and have a breakaway. As the ball touched down in his stick, Mike didn't see the Rams player come off the bench late. With a sickening thud Mike took the hit in the most vulnerable position possible — arms stretched above his head, looking back, catching the ball. As he crashed to the floor, the ball popped loose. The Rams player scooped it up and threw a long-range pass of his own to Taylor, who caught the Thunder off guard with the sudden change of direction. In all alone on Donnie, Taylor faked high and bounced a shot between his legs and into the net — 3–0 Rams.

Dazed, Mike sat on the floor as the Rams player who had hit him loomed over him. "Welcome back, homeboy!" the guy said, smirking. Turning, he jogged over to the Rams bench. WARCHUK was written across the shoulders of his jersey.

Stumbling to his feet, Mike headed back toward the Thunder bench. "Who the heck's that?" he asked as he ran past Cayln.

"Eric Warchuk. He's a really great player. Moved here from Vancouver a few months back."

"Well, he better keep his head up!" Mike shouted back.

"He's a good guy, Mike. It was a clean hit. He was just showing you that you have to keep your head up." Under all the anger and frustration, Mike knew Cayln was right. He likely would have done the same thing if he had a chance for a great hit like that. But it still sucked!

The rest of the period didn't go much better than the first few minutes. By the time the buzzer sounded to signal the period was over, the score was 7–0 for the Rams. The Thunder didn't even have a shot on net. Warchuk had three of the goals. The team sat dejectedly in silence on the floor along the boards, guzzling water during the break. Donnie seemed close to tears.

Ben walked back and forth, then halted in front of Mike. Catching his son's eye, he winked, then became very serious. "Mike, that has got to be the worst period of lacrosse I've ever seen you play. It was pathetic! You owe this team an apology. If you were trying as hard as everyone else, we'd be in this game instead of behind by seven. And what's this trying to win it all on your own crap? This is a team sport, and you know it. You're the only guy who's actually been in a game before, and instead of showing everyone else how to settle things down, you're setting the wrong example."

"Coach!"

Everyone turned to see Gwen standing at the end of the line of players sitting on the floor.

"We're all letting you down," Gwen said. "We all need to do better. We seem surprised at how fast this is and how good these guys are. We shouldn't be. We knew this wasn't going to be easy, and if we thought it was, we were dreaming. Mike might be trying to do too much, but we have to do more. Now let's go!" As if to emphasize her point, she slammed her stick against the boards and marched back to the bench.

The other players jumped to their feet, and with yells of encouragement, headed to the bench as the referee blew his whistle to announce the start of the second period.

"How you holding up, Donnie?" Ben asked as Donnie wandered over to put on his mask and gloves.

Donnie shook his head. "Jeez, I suck! I bet you're wishing Grant never got hurt and you didn't have a big fat goof in net like me."

Ben gripped Donnie by the shoulders and stopped him in his tracks. Standing over him, he gazed into the boy's enormous eyes. "Donnie, I wouldn't want anyone else in net but you. This isn't hockey. The scores are higher, and when a team like ours is adjusting, the goalie takes a bit of a beating. You're getting better with each minute of this game. Having you in net means a lot to this team. Now get in there and knock 'em dead."

Donnie's eyes narrowed to normal size, and he tightened his lips until they became a thin line. Determination in his face, he pulled his mask on and strode defiantly toward his net. "It's Donnie's turn now!" he growled.

The team settled down, and the second period was much better than the first. Donnie adjusted to the speed of the passes and began to make save after incredible save. Ben shifted things around and came up with player combinations that seemed to work well. He kept Mike at point with his basketball line of Mitchell and Tyler on crease. Bobby at point with

Gwen on crease worked extremely well, and he rotated Mark and Tommy at the other crease position. As shooters, he paired Joseph with Dennis and Billy with David. That seemed to create a strong balance.

With time winding down in the second period, the Rams had only scored one additional goal, but Warchuk was still doing a great job of getting under the Thunder players' skins. He was a strong, lean, quick player with fantastic stick skills. Warchuk was always in the action, and when he battled Joseph a little too vigorously and stripped him of the ball, the big boy lost his temper. Chasing Warchuk into the corner, Joseph levelled him with a check from behind and got a five-minute penalty.

Ben put out Ricky, Mitchell, Bobby, and David. Mitchell and Ricky did a sensational job of ragging the ball. With his long rock-star hair flowing behind his helmet, Mitchell frustrated the Rams as he dodged around the net. His hours of training for snowshoe races had given him a supply of energy that seemingly had no end. Ricky was like an evil twin but without the long hair. When the Rams did get the ball, Bobby and David did their bit defensively, and Donnie stopped everything that got past them. All the same it was five-on-four, and in lacrosse that made a huge difference in five minutes. The Rams scored two more goals before the end of the period to make it 10–0.

With a short bench of only twelve players, the Thunder were beginning to feel fatigue as they sat down for the break between the second and third periods. Ben got to his feet to provide some words of encouragement when a ruckus broke out near the closest gate leading onto the floor. All the players looked up as a face with a thick walrus-like moustache appeared through the Plexiglas.

The gate swung open, and Todd Lorenz marched across the floor. Patting Ben on the back, he turned and shook his head at the players. "That's got to be one of the best comeback periods of lacrosse I've ever seen. You guys ... and gal —" he winked at Gwen "— are amazing! Keep adjusting to the game and stay calm. You're incredible athletes. And you've got a terrific goalie in net." He looked at Donnie. "Where in the world did you come from? You must've been hiding when I was in Inuvik."

The players all smiled, including Donnie, who had seemed as if he were about to die a moment earlier.

"But, Mr. Lorenz ... Todd," Gwen said quietly, "isn't your son on the other team? What are you doing here?"

"Man, this isn't hockey or football or any other sport," Todd said. "This is lacrosse! In lacrosse we help each other out because it helps the game. And

the game is what we play for. You gotta love it!" He
grinned from ear to ear.

The referee blew his whistle, indicating the start
of the third period. The players stood and gathered
around Ben and Todd.

"Now put it in here, Thunder, and give 'em hell!"
Todd yelled.

"One, two, three, Inuvik!" the team shouted.

The third period was beautiful. Halfway through
no one had scored, and the play had shifted to a more
even distribution of shots on each net. With about
eight minutes left the Rams took a rare penalty, and
Ben called the players back to the bench.

"Okay, guys, let's really take our time and set this
up. I want Mike, Gwen, and Bobby up front. Mark, I
want you out with Joseph as shooters. Control that
ball, move it around, and shoot when you get your
chances. Let's go!"

The Rams won the faceoff, and Warchuk scooped
the ball up at full speed. Lifting his head, he was met
straight on by the Inuvialuit bowling ball. Mark had
read the play, and much like the earlier hit on Mike,
he clobbered the Rams player as soon as Warchuk
had the ball. Warchuk hit the floor hard, his head
snapping back as he fell. The ball popped out of his
stick, and Joseph scooped it up, quickly passing to

Bobby as he entered the Rams' zone.

Warchuk shook his head as he ran past Mark. "Nice hit."

The Rams set up their box as the Thunder moved the ball around the outside. Bobby passed back to Joseph, who moved it quickly to Mark. Mark threw the ball to the corner where Mike picked it up. The Thunder's captain faked a shot and passed to Mark on the point. Mark jogged behind the net, stopping just outside the crease near the post. He passed to Joseph, who quickly threw the ball to Bobby. Gwen had broken free and was cutting for the net. Bobby passed the ball as she rushed past Mike toward the other side of the net. The Rams' goalie, Kirk Miles, shifted across as Gwen caught the ball, expecting her to shoot. Mike stood ready, and when she passed the ball over her shoulder, he fired it into the open side of the net. The Thunder's players went wild on the bench as Bobby, Gwen, Mark, and Joseph mobbed Mike. It was 10–1 for the Rams, but the Thunder felt as if they had just won the championship.

"Whooooo!" rang out above the other polite cheers and clapping in the crowd. Turning toward the stands, the Thunder players spotted Todd Lorenz standing with both arms stretched above his head. Holding a thumb up, he nodded at the team.

Their first goal seemed to inspire the Thunder. They dominated the last five minutes of the game, winning every loose ball and getting some great chances on net. With one minute left in the game, once again they had the ball controlled in the Rams' zone. The clock was ticking down the final minute when Dennis fired a laser pass to Tommy in the corner. Faking toward the net, he ran behind and pulled back his stick, ready to pass to Gwen, who was streaking toward the net. Instead, he pulled his stick down, coiled his legs under his body, and launched himself into the air. Sailing over the crease horizontally, he caught Kirk by surprise and popped the ball into the far side of the net before landing on the floor. This time there were more than a few gasps from the crowd, and the applause was quite a bit louder.

The final score was 10–2, but the Thunder held the Rams scoreless for the entire third period and won some fans in the process. As the teams lined up and shook hands, the Rams stopped and talked to Mike and the other Inuvik players.

Warchuk stood next to Mike and slapped him on the back. "You're all right, man! You guys are gonna do okay in the tournament."

Mike grinned. "I can still feel that hit you gave me."

Warchuk groaned. "You can feel that hit? Jeez, my teeth are still loose from that Kikoak guy hitting me. Man, is he strong for his size."

Mike shook his head. "You have no idea."

Mike was proud of his team, but there wasn't much time to dwell on the finer points of this game. Tomorrow morning they played Leduc.

CHAPTER 24

The mood in the dressing room the next morning was light and fun. Tyler was dancing in the middle of the dressing room when Jimmy Quinlan came quietly though the door. Holding his fingers to his lips, he snuck up behind Tyler and jabbed him in the ribs. Tyler almost jumped out of his skin as the other boys killed themselves laughing.

"Hey, guys!" Jimmy said, waving.

"Hey, Jimmy!" they all called back.

"I hear you boys looked pretty good at the end of the game yesterday." Jimmy glanced around the room, then turned to Tommy. "And I hear the NLL scouts are looking for *you* because *you're* trying to take my job again."

Tommy shrugged and smiled.

Ben came through the door to the dressing room with Gwen who had put her equipment on in another area they had set aside for female players. She sat next to Mike.

"Look, everybody," Jimmy said, "Todd and Ben tell me you showed incredible courage yesterday, and an incredible will to keep going no matter what. You shut down the Rams in the third period. They're favoured to win this tournament. I think you have them looking over their shoulders now. If you win against Leduc, you can get into a rhythm that any other team is going to have trouble stopping. So have some fun, knock some Leduc players on their butts, and win this game!"

"Yay!" Donnie shouted in his usual overenthusiastic style.

"All right!" the other players cried, jumping to their feet and high-fiving Jimmy on the way out to the playing surface.

The game against Leduc was an entirely different story from the lopsided affair against the Rams the day before. On the third shift of the game the Thunder penned Leduc in its own end. Joseph, Dennis, Gwen, Bobby, and Mark moved the ball around the perimeter. Each time Joseph passed the ball, he moved a step closer to the Leduc net. Just as the thirty-second clock hit three seconds, he caught the ball, reared back, and fired. The goalie didn't even move as the ball ripped under his arm and into the net. The Thunder had their first lead of the tournament.

Joseph raised his arms and pumped his fists as his teammates rubbed the top of his helmet. There was a decent-sized crowd for a morning game, and the cheer that went up was loud. A lot of people had heard about their finish the day before and wanted to see the team from the Northwest Territories do well.

"Man, that felt good," Joseph said as he passed Mike on the shift change.

"Get used to it," Mike shot back. "I've got a feeling you're going to get a few more of those."

The period was close, but the Thunder had the edge. Bobby scored their second goal on a breakaway when a Leduc defender misjudged his, what Ben called, "put you to sleep" speed. Their third goal came on a nifty passing play between Mike, Mitchell, and Tyler that Mitchell finished with a nice bounce shot between the goalie's legs. It ended 3–1.

The second period was a back-and-forth affair that saw Mike and David score goals but Leduc answered with two of their own. The teams entered the third period with the score 5–3 for the Thunder.

Halfway through the third period, with the Thunder gaining momentum, the game took an ugly turn. Mark went into the corner with a Leduc player after a loose ball. With his amazing strength Mark held the much taller player off and battled until he had the ball. Suddenly, the Leduc player stopped, leaned close to Mark, and said something. Mark straightened and stared at the player in disbelief. The referee, who was close to the play, immediately shot his arm into the air to signal a penalty. Gwen had been hurtling in to help Mark, and as the referee readied himself to blow his whistle, she flew past, dropped her stick, and hit the Leduc player with a flurry of punches. The linesmen rushed in quickly to pull the players apart, but the damage had been done. Both the Leduc player and Gwen were sent to their dressing rooms, finished for a minimum of the rest of the game.

Mark trotted to the bench and immediately sat down facing away from the floor. Some of the other players tried to ask him what had happened, but he shook his head and looked away. After settling things at the penalty box, the referee headed over to explain the outcome to Ben.

The Leduc player received an initial technical penalty for making a racist comment to Mark. He also got a roughing penalty and a game misconduct for fighting.

Gwen received a game misconduct for fighting. The referee continued to explain that there would have to be a disciplinary meeting after the game to decide if any further action, including suspensions, would be made. The final result was a power play for the Thunder.

Ben sidled over to Mark. "Are you okay, son?"

Mark raised his head. "Yeah, I guess I wasn't expecting something like that."

"It's just a sign of stupidity and fear," Ben said. "When ignorant people feel cornered or insecure, or don't understand something, they turn to racism. What Gwen did wasn't right, either. I know she's emotional and her first reaction was to lash out, but all that did was hurt us. Now we're without a great player. Guys like that Leduc player always get what's coming to them, and it's going to be dealt with. Don't let one guy's idiocy spoil lacrosse for you. We're going to win this game, so enjoy it. All right?"

Mark held Ben's gaze for a moment. Then he nodded and stood to cheer his teammates on.

The penalty killed Leduc's chances as the Thunder scored and continued to pick up steam. The game ended with a final score of 8–3. The Thunder had their first win!

CHAPTER 25

The Thunder played their third game that afternoon. Ben had a meeting with tournament officials and
informed the boys there was good and bad news. The
Leduc player was suspended from any further play in
the tournament. There was a strong chance he would
be suspended from league play for the rest of the year.
The bad news was that Gwen had been suspended for
one game. Given the circumstances and the fact that
she hadn't dropped her gloves, the tournament execu-
tive had made the one-game ruling. With a bench that
had started out short, and having played a game that
morning, the suspension really hurt. Being another
player down meant the rest of the team would be on
the floor almost non-stop.

Although they were short a player, the Thunder didn't miss a beat. As Jimmy Quinlan had said, they'd hit a rhythm. It seemed the thrill of their first win, the adversity of the Leduc game, and the necessity of competing with fewer players than any other team in the tournament gave them extra strength and adrenaline. The game was never in jeopardy, and they beat the Warriors 6–4.

With Gwen back for their fourth game, they defeated a pesky Red Deer team 8–6. A record of three wins and one loss put them in the playoff round. The Edmonton Blues would be their next opponents, while the Rams were up against Fort Saskatchewan. The winners of those two matches would play for the gold medal.

The game against the Blues was an incredible battle. The first two periods saw the teams trade goal for goal. Late in the second period, Mark scored a goal that had everyone in the stands on their feet. Taking a pass at centre floor, he bowled over an attacker who tried to squeeze him into the boards. After cutting to the middle, he faked a pass to Bobby and spun away from a second Blues defender. Picking up speed, he charged straight for the net. Two Blues players hit him hard from each side as he neared the top of the crease. Like a powerful fullback, he kept his legs moving and managed two more steps before he fired the ball into the bottom corner of the net as he fell.

The Thunder entered the third period with a 5–4 lead. Donnie did the rest. No matter what they tried, the Blues couldn't score. With every kick and every lunge across the net, Donnie got stronger.

With one minute left in the game the Blues pulled their goalie for a sixth attacker. As time wound down, they peppered Donnie only to be met with frustration. On one last attack by the Blues, Donnie did the final damage. Gaining control of the ball after stopping a shot, he lobbed it the length of the floor where it took three bounces and lazily floated into the empty net. The game was over — Thunder 6, Blues 4. Donnie was so excited at not only winning the game but scoring a goal that he was literally dancing on the spot as the rest of the team mobbed him in front of the net.

The boys received word that the Rams had won their game against Fort Saskatchewan, so it would be an Inuvik–St. Albert rematch in the final. But this time it would be a very different Inuvik team playing against the Rams.

CHAPTER 26

The afternoon of the championship game Ben walked into the boys' dressing room with Gwen and found everyone deathly quiet.

"I don't think there's an empty seat out there," Gwen said, sitting beside Mike. "I even saw TV cameras along one side of the arena."

Donnie seemed startled. "TV cameras?"

Ben nodded. "Two of the local stations have cameras here for the game. We can watch the highlights of our win tonight."

Some of the players had smiles pasted on their faces, but they were tight-lipped, short-lived ones. Clearing his throat, Ben moved to the centre of the room. As he prepared to speak, Mike stood and walked over to his father. "I've got something to say."

Ben stepped off to the side. "Go ahead, Mike."

"Well, I'm not great at this, guys, but we've got an amazing team. We're all pretty quiet right now, and that's good because we need to focus. And we're likely a little nervous, but I bet the guys in the Rams' dressing room are even more nervous. When we put this team together, it was great, but I didn't really think we'd do much. I figured we'd come out here and get killed by everybody but that it would be fun to play lacrosse again. Then I saw how incredible all of you are and I knew we had a chance."

Mike paused for a moment, then continued. "Man, we've only lost one game! The Rams know that, and they've seen us get better every time we play. The pressure's on them in front of their home crowd. We're just a bunch of newbies from the North who weren't supposed to win a single game. Now look at us. I bet when we run onto the floor in a few minutes the crowd's going to cheer just as loud for us as they do for St. Albert. And they should. We're good, man! We're better than good. We're exciting to watch. We're a team, and we have fun when we play. So let's put it together, keep it going, and win this for Inuvik!"

"*Yaaaaaa!*" The players jumped to their feet and started to put on their helmets and gloves. Ben led the way into the tunnel to the playing surface, with Donnie close behind and then the other players. They heard a cheer as they opened the door, signalling that the Rams had taken the floor. Ben stood aside, and as Donnie burst out of the tunnel with the other players behind him, another cheer rose from the stands. To Mike it sounded even louder than the one the Rams had received a few minutes ago.

Mike tried to avoid looking at the Rams' end of the floor as the Thunder conducted warm-up drills and took shots at Donnie. The one time he did glance back he saw Warchuk standing at centre floor. Their eyes met, and after what seemed a long couple of seconds, the Rams player nodded slightly. Mike returned the nod courteously, but knew that this game was going to be out-and-out war.

When the referee blew his whistle, the teams gathered in front of their benches and gave one last cheer before the game began. Mike was starting with Mitchell and Tyler, along with Joseph and Dennis as shooters. They faced Ryan, Taylor, Eric Warchuk, Spencer, and Matt Borodawka. Matt was a big, aggressive shooter who loved to run the ball up the floor.

"Hey, Mike," Ryan said as they came together for the faceoff.

"Hey, yourself," Mike said.

"You ready for this?"

"Yeah, Ryan, it should be fun. And you guys won't be scoring ten goals this time."

As he knelt for the faceoff, Ryan shrugged. "We'll see."

Ryan cleanly won the faceoff, but Mitchell out-hustled Taylor and scooped up the ball. Dodging a check from Matt, he tossed a quick pass to Mike, who slowed the tempo down and walked the ball into the Rams' zone. Keeping an eye on the thirty-second clock, the Thunder moved the ball around the outside. With Tyler holding the ball in the corner, the middle opened up. Joseph broke for the net, yelling for the ball. As the pass sank into the basket of his stick, he drew back and fired. Kirk Miles didn't see the shot, but it was slightly off target and struck the post with a thud, then ricocheted back toward the Thunder's end with incredible velocity.

Everyone was caught off guard, and with both Joseph and Dennis in deep, Warchuk was after the ball in a flash. Seeing the ball bouncing toward him from the Rams' end with Warchuk in hot pursuit, Donnie charged out of his net on a collision course with the Rams player. Just before they collided, Warchuk's outstretched stick swept the ball up as he dodged Donnie's flailing body. Regaining his balance, Warchuk jogged in all alone and lightly shot the ball into the empty net. As the crowd cheered, Warchuk stood beside the net with his arms in the air. With just under a minute gone on the clock, the Rams were up 1–0. Donnie slammed his stick against the floor in frustration as he marched back to his net.

"Change it up!" Ben shouted. "Let's all settle down and get that one back!"

This time Bobby won the faceoff, and Mark scooped up the ball. Passing it to Gwen, he ran to the front of the net and battled with Scott Sutherland for position. Scott was much taller, but he found Mark almost impossible to budge. Gwen threw the ball back to Billy, who passed it across to David. David in turn lobbed the ball quickly to Gwen. Pretending to pass, Gwen dodged a check and sprinted for the net. She faked a shot, then moved as if she were going to pass over her shoulder. When Kirk went for the fake, she fired the ball into the top corner of the net. The game was tied. All Kirk could do was shake his head.

The rest of the first period proved to be a defensive struggle, with both Donnie and Kirk making several beautiful saves. Ryan scored a nice one for the Rams when he took a pass from Brady and popped the ball behind Donnie with a quick stick shot. Joseph answered back for the Thunder just before the end of the period with a shot so hard that it spun the stick out of Kirk's hands before squirting between his pads and into the net.

With the score tied 2–2, both teams were cautious at the beginning of the second period. The tide shifted in favour of the Thunder when Tyler laid out Cayln Butz with an unbelievable hit. Despite a slender build, much like Cayln's, Tyler loved to hit, and when he caught Cayln with his head down, he unloaded. Then Spencer came in late for the Rams and flattened Tyler with a solid check. The referee's arm immediately shot up, and Spencer went to the penalty box for two minutes.

Ben put Mike, Gwen, Tommy, Bobby, and Joseph on the floor. Setting up in the Rams' zone, they moved the ball quickly around the outside. Gwen and Tommy had adjusted quickly to the idea of staying in motion and presented Kirk with a steady flow of moment in front of his net. Once again, Joseph moved in closer after every pass. Finally, receiving the ball once more from Bobby, he reared back for a shot. Remembering the last rocket Joseph launched at Kirk, the Rams seemed to freeze. This time Joseph took a little bit off the ball and fired wide to Mike, who was standing at the edge of the crease. As the ball entered his pocket, Mike fired it into the net.

That goal seemed to energize the Thunder, and even though the Rams were back at full strength, Mike and his team took control and peppered Kirk with shot after shot. It finally paid off when an off-speed rocket by Ricky Alexie fooled Kirk and got behind him into the net. The period ended with the score 4–2 for the Thunder.

Ben didn't have to say much between periods. The team was tired, and the test in the third and final period would be whether they could outlast the fresher legs on the Rams' squad. With three full lines St. Albert had a distinct advantage.

The first five minutes of the last period had no rhythm for either team. There were missed passes and shots, with a true lack of ball control by both squads. Donnie was sensational and frustrated the Rams at every opportunity. And during the entire tournament his passes up the floor had become much more accurate with each game. That made it all the more devastating when Donnie attempted to lob the ball to Joseph at the side of the net and Warchuk intercepted it. Diving back, Donnie caught part of the shot, but it wasn't enough. The score was now 4–3 for the Thunder.

That goal invigorated the Rams, and they relentlessly attacked the Thunder, who were now starting to display fatigue. Time after time the Rams ran up the floor with the Inuvik players trying to match them stride for stride. With eight minutes left in the game, the Thunder tried to hold on with mounting desperation. Mike had Spencer lined up for a hit in the corner and braced himself for contact as he lunged. Spencer turned away to avoid the check, and though he tried to adjust, Mike couldn't stop. He struck Spencer flush in the back, and they both tumbled to the floor.

Mike heard the referee's whistle, and glancing up, saw his arm in the air. Pointing at Mike, he shouted, "Five minutes for hitting from behind!" Mike's heart sank.

Enraged, Ben jumped onto the bench and let the referee know how bad a call he'd made.

"One more word, Coach," the referee warned, "and not only will your team go down another man for a technical, but you'll be out of the game, too."

Ben hopped back behind the bench, still livid. Collecting his thoughts, he sent Joseph, Ricky, Mitchell, and Bobby onto the floor. All Mike could do was sit in the penalty box and blame himself for a stupid penalty.

The Rams' power play started slow, and several times the Thunder stole the ball, allowing Mitchell to rag it and waste time, frustrating the Rams to no end. But it couldn't last. The Thunder were just too tired. Brady finally broke free in the corner and outraced

Gwen to the front of the net, depositing the ball low on Donnie's stick side. The game was tied 4–4, and the penalty still wasn't over.

St. Albert could smell blood. Gaining control of the ball, the Rams set up once more in the Thunder's end. They passed the ball quickly around the perimeter, forcing the weary Thunder players out of position. With only seconds left in Mike's penalty, Scott ripped a shot over Donnie's shoulder and into the net. Donnie slumped to the floor, and the crowd went wild as the Rams mobbed Scott.

With three minutes left and the score 5–4 for the Rams, St. Albert wasn't taking any chances. The Rams stayed aggressive to pressure the Thunder, who continued to flag but also kept two men well back at all times. As the clock wound down, the Thunder's spirits began to sag, and Mike felt as if he were going to be sick.

Ben called a timeout with fifty seconds remaining on the clock. "Okay, boys, this is it. As soon as play starts, I want someone to pressure the ball carrier immediately if they get possession. Donnie, if we get possession, I want you to hustle to the bench. Got it?" Donnie nodded, his face slick with sweat. "I want Mike, Joseph, Gwen, Tommy, and Bobby on the floor. Mark, I want you ready to get out there when Donnie comes to the bench." Ben studied the faces in front of him. "Are we ready?"

"Yeah," the team said not too enthusiastically.

"Are we ready?" Ben shouted again, this time at the top of his lungs.

"Yeah!" the team shouted a lot louder.

The referee blew his whistle, and the teams walked back onto the floor. When the Rams were ready, the referee tossed Spencer the ball and blew the game back into play. Spencer took his time moving, and Bobby was all over him quickly, so he passed the ball to Cayln, who jogged into the Thunder's zone. Mike and Gwen ran at Cayln with their sticks in the air. Cayln forced a bounce pass between them to Ryan in the corner, but Joseph was too quick. With his long reach he lunged and tipped the pass away. Bobby scooped up the ball, stopped behind the net, and spotted Tommy breaking up the left side.

"Here, here!" Tommy cried.

Bobby threw a perfect pass that Tommy caught on the fly. Only Eric Warchuk stood between him and the Rams' net. Bending his knees, the Rams defender hunched over, waiting for Tommy to try to get by.

With a slight hesitation and a hop, Tommy broke into an all-out sprint directly at Warchuk. As Tommy continued to gain speed, Warchuk braced himself for the crash and crouched lower.

"Oh, man, he's not ..." Mike whispered to no one in particular.

Gwen gasped beside him. "Jeez, I think he is!"

Just as Warchuk leaned forward to meet the oncoming charge, Tommy left his feet. Pulling his legs close to his body, he sailed over Warchuk's head, clearing the helmet of the Rams player easily. Unable to pull back, Warchuk fell forward onto the floor as Tommy landed and continued to run. In all alone on Kirk, he faked high and shot low on the startled goalie. Kirk dropped with the shot, closing his pads and squeezing the ball. Tommy stopped by the net and watched, thrusting his arms into the air as the ball trickled from beneath Kirk and into the net. Catching up to the play, the referee threw both his arms up, indicating a goal. The arena erupted in cheers and a babble of excited conversations as people attempted to absorb in disbelief what they had just seen. The Thunder swarmed Tommy as he ran to the bench. The score was 5–5 with fifteen seconds left on the clock.

Ben left the same line on the floor to face the final seconds against the Rams, and Mike moved into the faceoff circle with Ryan once more.

Ryan shook his head as they knelt. "That was unbelievable!"

Mike nodded. "You should see the guy when he plays basketball."

The referee stepped back and blew his whistle. Ryan and Mike pushed down with all their might to gain enough leverage to win control of the ball. Finally, Mike drew it out and to the side where Gwen picked it up and ran toward the Rams' zone. Turning around anxiously, she hesitated, then passed back to Joseph, who fired a blistering shot that missed the net as the buzzer sounded to end the third period. Overtime!

The referee explained to the teams that they would play a ten-minute sudden-death overtime period. If the game wasn't settled after that, there would be a shootout.

Ben studied the tired faces of his players. "Look, gang, you've played harder than any team I've ever coached. Be proud. No one expected a team from Inuvik to win a single game. We're playing overtime in the gold-medal championship. Can you win the next ten minutes?"

"*Yeah!*"

"Can you win the game?"

"*Yeah!*"

"Okay. Let's go with the same line, but, Mark, I want you out for Tommy."

Mike slowly walked to the faceoff circle where Ryan already stood. "Do you believe this, man?"

"You guys are truly awesome," Ryan said. "Let's hope the winner's a good goal."

The two friends exchanged fist bumps and knelt one more time. When the referee blew his whistle, Ryan dug hard and drew the ball to the side out of the faceoff circle. Bobby darted after the ball and snagged it in his stick. First possession belonged to the Thunder!

Bobby passed to Gwen, who threw the ball over to Mike as he jogged into the Rams' zone. Setting up their box, the Rams thrust their sticks into the air, trying to thwart any pass. Mike threw the ball to Joseph, who drew back to shoot, but then passed to Mark. Mark lunged as if to run at the net but passed to Bobby at the side of the net. Bobby one-timed it over to Mike, who fired away. Kirk flicked out his leg and kicked the ball to the corner. Scooping up the ball, Scott led the Rams' attack up the floor.

Hustling back, the Thunder set up a box of their own as the Rams manoeuvred the ball around the outside. With the shot clock down to fifteen seconds, Cayln threw a pick for Ryan in the corner. Cutting across hard to the goal, Ryan ripped a shot at the bottom corner of the net. Donnie kicked his leg out in dramatic fashion, and the ball hit his pad. It popped off the hard plastic and struck Mark in the back of the leg, bouncing toward the net. Horrified, Donnie and the rest of the Thunder team watched as the ball dribbled back into the far corner of the net. The Rams' bench exploded as gloves and helmets flew into the air. Donnie flopped onto his back and covered the cage of his mask with both hands as he started to cry.

The Thunder were heartbroken! They stood dumbstruck as the Rams celebrated.

Breaking away from the revelry, Ryan Domino jogged to the Thunder net. "Hey, Donnie, isn't it?"

Donnie peered out from between his gloves. "Yeah."

"You played one incredible game, and if it wasn't for my one fluky goal, you guys would've likely won. You kept your team in there, and you're one of the best goalies I've ever seen." Ryan bent over and extended his hand to the big boy. Slowly, Donnie sat up, gripped Ryan's hand, and hoisted himself to his feet.

The rest of the Rams joined Ryan in the Thunder's zone. Without waiting for the traditional lineup at centre floor, they began to shake hands and exchange congratulations.

"That has got to be the most amazing move I've never seen," Warchuk said to Tommy. "I closed my eyes because I thought we were going to hit so hard. I open them, and you've jumped clear over my head!"

Tommy couldn't help but smile. "Thanks, man. You're an incredible player, too. We learned a lot playing against you guys."

Todd Lorenz and Jimmy Quinlan made their way onto the floor, and along with Ben, huddled the players together.

Jimmy shook his head at Tommy. "Okay, man, now I've seen everything. The Rush just called and told me I've been traded. They want to sign you to a long-term contract."

Most of the team managed to smile, and the mood began to lighten.

"Boys, and Gwen," Todd said, "you've done yourselves proud. You've done the game of lacrosse proud. Watching you play made me realize I'm the luckiest guy alive to be part of this great game. And I hope you all feel the same way. No one will ever forget Arctic Thunder."

After the officials brought the championship trophy onto the floor and presented it to Ryan, Spencer, and Eric, they waved the Thunder players over. Together the two teams jogged around the rink, with everyone on both sides taking turns carrying the hardware. The fans stood and cheered as both teams shared the trophy.

When they stopped, the Rams insisted that a picture be taken of both teams clustered around the trophy. With some players sprawled on the floor, others kneeling, and a few standing in the back, the party continued.

Mike felt arms loop around his neck from the left and right. Gwen and Joseph both smiled at him widely as they pushed in close. Mike rumpled Donnie's hair as he crouched in front of the other players, and there was no way to describe the expression of happiness that filled those huge eyes.

As the cameras flashed, Mike held his index finger above his head, much as he had more than a year ago at the provincials. This time it felt even more like a victory.

EPILOGUE

Mike sat quietly and glanced out the window of the plane to Inuvik. They were above the clouds, and all he could see was a white blanket below him. He smiled and contemplated the interior of the cabin. Donnie was sitting next to him, head slightly flopped to one side, sound asleep. The silver medal they won was still hanging loosely around Donnie's neck.

Leaning forward, Mike looked across the aisle to where Tommy, Bobby, and Joseph sat. It was quite clear that all three had fallen asleep, as well. Lifting himself half out of his seat, Mike peered over the heads in front of him and across the aisle a couple of rows up. Gwen turned and caught his eye. Smiling, she gave him a little wave that he returned before relaxing and sitting back down.

Warmth filled Mike's chest, and he turned back to the window, not knowing whether to laugh or cry. He knew where he belonged now and what made him happy. Most of all, he knew what was important in life. Tipping his head back, he closed his eyes and smiled. "*Quyanaq*, Victor," he said out loud. "*Quyanainni*. Thank you."

ALSO BY
ROBERT FEAGAN

Napachee
978-1-55002-636-8
$11.99

Napachee is tired of Sachs Harbour, Northwest
Territories. He is weary of the traditional Inuit hunt
and of fighting with his father, who shuns snowmobiles for dog sleds and tents for igloos. When two
men from the Edmonton zoo fly in to capture a polar
bear cub, Napachee spies his chance at a trip to the
big city, but soon discovers that life there is not what
he had expected.

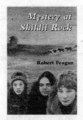

Mystery at Shildii Rock
978-1-55002-668-9
$11.99

To the Gwich'in First Nation, Shildii Rock near Fort McPherson in the Northwest Territories is a place of deep mythological significance. When twelve-year-old Robin Harris, the son of a Royal Canadian Mounted Police officer, spots someone on the rock staring at him, he just knows something is wrong. Robin and his friend Wayne Reindeer, a Gwich'in youth, set out to discover what's going on and to gain the respect of their fathers. Their journey is besieged by challenges, and when murder comes their way, Robin and Wayne realize it's too late to turn back. Will the boys unlock the secrets of Shildii Rock in time? Or will they, too, fall victim to a killer?